CRESTFALLEN

SPELLCREST ACADEMY, BOOK 2

MICHAEL PIERCE

"**A**re you really gonna wear that tonight?" Trish asked when Ben exited the bedroom.

Ben glanced down at his jeans and button-down flannel shirt, seemingly perplexed. "Yeah; why?"

"That shirt has a hole in the elbow."

"I like this shirt."

"And it's nice for lounging around the apartment and running errands, but not going out for New Year's Eve." Trish waddled up to him in a tight black dress that was all looks and no function, ushering him back into the bedroom.

"I think it's fine," I said, though I knew my opinion didn't matter. Actually, it was discouraged.

Trish didn't even acknowledge my statement. "Why didn't you put on the shirt I'd laid out for you?" Then the two of them disappeared into the bedroom while I was forced to wait patiently on the couch.

My patience had grown by leaps and bounds since arriving back in Hollywood.

Ben wasn't really happy with his new girlfriend, even though he said he was. He needed someone to take care of him. And that was exactly who she was —a controlling mother bird. She regulated everything in his life to keep him clean and in line—and *hers*. It was obvious she saw me as a threat, not because he was falling for me, but because I challenged her control.

And he was naive enough to think we'd get along.

I couldn't deny she was good for keeping him clean, which was what he needed most when I left and he met her. He needed someone because I couldn't be there for him. But now that I was back, well... let's just say I wasn't going to let her freakin' boss me around. Lately, it seemed like everywhere I went, I was getting hit with freshman status.

I'd spent the holidays sleeping on the living room couch. There was only the one bedroom and I had nowhere else to go, so I couldn't afford to be picky. In truth, the couch was quite comfortable, it just didn't lend itself to much privacy—not to mention the single bathroom, which was an en suite to the bedroom. We pretty much had to share everything.

And if Trish had been less territorial, I would have been cooler with the whole situation. I'd been getting along well sharing a room with Nym and Razielle for several months, so I was confident the problem wasn't all me. I also knew that Ben had to tread lightly because Trish was his girlfriend and I was a household guest. Ben was the only reason I hadn't yet slapped her across the face or put a laxative in her herbal tea.

I was able to finagle my old job back at the restaurant, but I didn't return to school. After the New Year, I planned to schedule the GED and get on with my life. Now I was able to work all the time, not simply around my school schedule. So, I did, to keep myself out of the apartment as much as possible and save up some money. And as I worked more regularly, I settled into what most people would consider a normal routine... well, as normal as one could be, living with a pseudo-older brother and his bitchy girlfriend.

My normal was trying to forget all about magic and what it had cost me. It had essentially stolen my whole family from me. My parents' souls were trapped in crystals and Finley had ripped my needle from my finger. I had no more supernatural abilities outside of efficient packing—Finley had seen to that —so I didn't belong in that world any longer. I didn't even want to be reminded of it.

While I was waiting for the old married couple to agree on what constituted appropriate club attire, I received a text from Nym, wishing me a Happy New

Year. Her family lived on the East Coast and it was nearly midnight over there.

It wasn't unusual to receive texts from Razielle or Nym. On several occasions, Razielle had even tried to convince me to fly out to her parents' house in San Francisco. I typically dodged the offer with a non-answer. However, I convinced myself that my supernatural friends were regular girlfriends I'd once shared a room with at one of the many group homes. I tried to completely erase from my mind what they really were—a half-elf and a Nephilim— because those kinds of beings simply didn't exist in the real world. Ask anyone.

I held the phone out for a selfie and sent it to Nym, wishing her a Happy New Year as well. I thought she'd get a kick out of me wearing the same outfit I'd worn for the Halloween festival at Spell-crest Village, a crimson corset top and black leather pants. I even had the same heels, though she couldn't see those in the picture. The noticeable difference was the octagram tattoo that was no longer emblazoned across my chest, which had been on full display at Halloween. Now I had no tattoo or soul crystal necklace. See... normal.

Nym texted back a picture of herself at the house party she was at. Though I wouldn't really call it a house. Her parents owned an estate in the Hamptons, so all of their family friends were rich. And Nym wasn't wearing anything close to what Razielle and I had dressed her up in for Halloween. Her scandalous dress was traded in for nicely-tailored slacks and a cardigan. Her pointy ears stuck wistfully out of her strawberry blond hair. She looked exactly like the Nym we all knew and loved.

"See, doesn't that look *so* much better?" Trish asked as the two of them exited the bedroom.

"It's stiff," Ben complained as he walked in my direction. He stopped and did a little twirl.

"No holes," I said. "How very grown up of you."

"It's like you've never owned new clothes before," Trish said and grabbed a reusable water bottle from the fridge.

"Not many," Ben said. I'd known he'd bought much of his clothing from thrift stores, though he did have a few hookups at specialty clothing stores. It was more that he just didn't want to buy new clothes. He still had hand-me-downs from our last group home together.

"Maeve, you have your fake ID?" Trish asked, strolling back into the living room.

"It's not fake. It just doesn't have my real age," I said, sourly, finishing up a text to Nym.

"Then it's fake, but whatever. How old does it say you are?"

"Twenty-five."

"You can't pass for twenty-five."

"It's worked before," I shot back, even though I hadn't actually been carded for anything yet. Ben had put me on the list of a few clubs he DJed at, sneaking me in the back door. And each time I'd gone up to a bar to order a drink, it had been a soda or water. I wasn't going to start drinking alcohol just because my license said I could. I didn't need that extra craziness in my life; I had enough with Trish.

"Well, if you don't get in, then you're on your own," Trish said, grabbing a black clutch from the dining room table. "Shall we?" She looped her arm through Ben's and gave an exaggerated gesture for me to get off my lazy ass.

Why'd I even agree to come tonight?

"Let's go set the world on fire," Ben said with a mischievous smile. It was little looks like this that reminded me of him before Trish.

On the way down, Ben called an Uber—not because the club we were going to was far, but because the one thing Trish and I agreed on was not wanting to walk more than a block in heels.

There were so many drivers out tonight, our car was practically waiting for us by the time we reached the sidewalk. As Ben held the door open, Trish pushed me in first, followed by her, so I wasn't able to sit beside him. The three of us were crammed into the back of a Prius, and I wasn't exactly keen on Trish's leg being pushed against mine. Luckily, I wasn't wearing a skirt too.

Even though the venue was literally a half mile away, it took us over ten minutes to get there. Hollywood Boulevard traffic was always bad, but a typical weekend night couldn't compare to New Year's Eve.

Because every place would be at capacity tonight, Trish had splurged to get us VIP tickets, so we could bypass the long line and get access to the lounge inside where we might actually have a chance to sit down.

To Trish's disdain, I floated right past security. The guy didn't even take a second look at my license. I smiled brightly, then glanced over at Trish who was clenching her jaw, holding tightly to Ben's arm.

Once we were inside, I let any homicidal thoughts of Trish subside as I was overtaken by the pounding music and the sea of beautiful people. I could find someone here who could make me forget all about Devon Christi. I still couldn't forgive him for keeping the secret of my parents from me. I'd felt like he'd betrayed me almost as much as Finley. My feelings were probably hypocritical, but I still felt justified in my resentment.

The fact was, after everything we'd been through, he hadn't tried to contact me once since I'd left. He was obviously over me. He'd said our connection wasn't based off the crystals of my parents—since we'd each had one—but his actions once I was gone spoke louder than his words from the last time we were together in the Crystal Crypt.

Devon not coming after me proved there had been no real connection between us. He didn't really care about me... or love me. And I wasn't going to pine over some arrogant asshole from a world I no longer belonged to. That magical world was dead to me. So was Devon and Finley and—I made exceptions for Nym and Razielle. But like I said, I no longer thought of them as magical beings.

The three of us hit the dance floor. At first, I was just dancing with myself, but over time found myself pulled toward different guys who seemed to have also come stag. Some of them got a little handsy, but I wanted to forget about the fact that I didn't have anyone and just went with the flow. It was when a guy wanted to lead me off the dance floor to buy me a drink or introduce me to his friends or make a move on one of the couches, that I drew the line. I just wanted to keep dancing and there seemed to always be another guy ready to take the last one's place.

I lost sight of Ben and Trish several times, but I could understand they wanted their own space. I did too. When I needed a break, I headed over to the bar and requested a water. One guy followed and tried to convince me I needed something a little stronger.

"You're right," I said. "Scrawny guys don't really do it for me." I sipped from the black straw and gazed up at him through my eyelashes, flashing an innocent smile.

"You're a bitch," he snapped and stormed off into the everchanging crowd.

Yeah; there's that.

I downed the rest of my water and headed back onto the dance floor, when I caught a glimpse of Ben making his way toward me.

"There you are," he shouted while he was still a way off. "I've been looking all over for you."

"Where's Trish?"

"Guarding the couch I was able to snag. Come on. It's nearly midnight." He grabbed my hand, which at first felt awkward, and led me through the crowd. I was tugged through groups of people that did *not* want to be separated. But we were gone before anyone had a chance to protest.

When we reached the VIP lounge, Ben dropped my hand and guided me to the couch that Trish seemed to be guarding with her life. There were couples and small groups milling about nearby, ready to pounce at the first sign of Trish abandoning her post.

Then on the end table, I noticed three glasses of champagne.

"Have a seat," Ben said. "I'm sure you'd like to get off your feet for a few minutes."

I couldn't argue with that—though I could keep my distance from Trish. I could also question whether or not those glasses were ours. "What are those?"

Ben gestured to the glasses. "They're for midnight. I had to get them early, so sorry if it's a little warm. But look at the bars now. Plenty of people aren't going to make it before midnight."

"Are you sure that's a good idea?" I asked.

"It's a special night. One glass won't hurt." He glanced down at Trish, who didn't look like she agreed, but also didn't correct him for once in her life. "We need to celebrate."

I didn't know what Trish had seen with him, but I'd seen enough to know this was a dangerous road. Maybe nothing would happen tonight, but it was opening the door to fall back into old patterns.

When the music stopped and the countdown began, Ben grabbed all three glasses and handed them out. The chorus of the crowd grew louder as we all approached *one*, then a blinding lightshow erupted, timed to the sounds of fireworks as we all shouted, "Happy New Year!"

The three of us clinked glasses. I brought mine to my lips and tipped it back, but stopped the champagne from passing my lips.

Ben and Trish kissed, and with his hand holding the flute positioned around her back, I noticed it was already empty. As soon as they parted, Ben pushed over to me and gave me a tight squeeze.

"Happy New Year," he said into my ear. "It's going to be a great one; I can feel it." And at that very moment, Trish's gaze was burning a hole into his back.

When he let go, he remained standing between us

two girls, his attention oscillating back and forth. "Are you going to drink that?" Ben finally asked me.

"I am," I lied and brought the flute to my lips again. I'd have to spill some behind the couch before too long.

"Anyone want anything else?"

Trish shook her head, still sipping from her glass.

"Okay. I'll be right back," he said and walked off into the crowd, still clutching the empty flute.

"I can't believe you're okay with this," I snapped at Trish.

"Like he said, one's not a big deal," she said, continuing to drink her champagne.

"You're assuming he's stopping at one."

CHAPTER 2

"*I*'m so sorry," Ben cried as Trish and I literally dragged him out of the club.

I didn't know how many drinks he had, but it didn't matter. He'd disappeared several more times since midnight. He didn't seem terribly bad until it was too late, and whatever else he'd drunk finally caught up with him.

He had an arm around each one of our shoulders, and we fought to keep him upright as we flooded the sidewalk of Hollywood Boulevard with countless other inebriated clubgoers. The street was still filled with cars trying to avoid the hordes of pedestrians. Honking and hollering filled the early-morning air like battle cries.

"I think I'm gonna throw up," Ben said, then started to heave.

I aimed him away from the street and helped him

to his knees. Trish knelt beside him, losing a heel in the process, and rubbed his back as he vomited all over the sidewalk.

Passersby hooted and laughed at Ben for not being able to handle his liquor. However, as was usually the case, outsiders looking in didn't know what was really going on, only what they saw, which was only a small part of the whole picture. I flipped off a few of the more raucous ones, but all that did was egg them on.

"I'm sorry, guys," Ben said again once he was done spewing his guts onto the concrete.

"Let's just get you home," I said, checking my phone for an Uber update. Per the app, our car was less than five minutes away. Just enough time to get Ben back on his feet.

"Do you feel any better?" Trish asked.

"Loads," Ben said, then laughed. "I can taste it in my nose. Still kinda bubbly."

"That's so gross."

Then I laughed from Trish's exaggerated grimace. At least Ben was still in relatively good spirits. And there was nothing I'd have to dump down the drain when we got home, either. All he'd have to do was sleep it off, then we'd see how irate Trish was in the morning once he'd sobered up. And if it came to that, I'd jump into the fight as well, blaming her for being an enabler. Then we'd really see what kind of shit hit the fan. I guessed I'd better get a good night's sleep as well.

I spotted the black Murano that was picking us up and ran over to it before anyone had the bright idea to steal it from us. I'd be so pissed if I was charged for a ride I wasn't in.

Holding open the back door of the SUV, I whistled and waved to Trish to get her attention. She carefully hobbled over with Ben's arm draped around her shoulder. As they approached, Ben spit on the sidewalk, then wiped his mouth with the sleeve of his nice new shirt.

"Get in," Trish barked at me.

I was tempted to argue, but thought I should save my energy for tomorrow. So, I complied and climbed into the backseat of the SUV, scooting to the far end of the leather bench seat as Ben crawled in behind me.

The driver's concerned eyes appeared in the rearview mirror. "Nobody better throw up in my car," he warned.

I punched the button to lower my window. "No one's going to throw up."

"I already did that," Ben said, sounding oddly proud of himself.

"Maybe you should keep some barf bags in your car if you're going to be picking people up at 2 a.m.," Trish said as Ben laid his head on her shoulder.

"I love you," Ben slurred in a way that made it

sound like one long word. It was the first time I'd heard him say that to her. I didn't know if it was something they were saying to each other now or if it was just drunk Ben talking, in which case, he wouldn't remember in the morning.

The Murano pushed into traffic, turned at the next light, and proceeded to circle around to our apartment complex by way of back streets.

At one of the stop-sign intersections, I looked up at the old Victorian house on the corner and realized it had been where I'd found Helena—the dying old woman who'd given me her needle. I'd found her in a heap on the grass, I passed out after she stabbed me with the needle, and when I awoke to the downcast faces of paramedics surrounding me, Helena had vanished. This was another reminder of the magical world I wanted to forget.

"Oh God!" Ben blurted out, then proceeded to climb over me and hang his head out the open window as he expelled more of the night's celebratory drinks.

"Watch your knees!" I exclaimed and swatted at his legs to keep them from digging into my thighs.

The car continued down the street at an accelerated pace as Ben continued to heave, his whole body convulsing over me. All I could do was sit there and wait for him to finish.

"You told me no one would throw up," the driver said, angrily.

"And none of it's in the car," I said.

By the time we reached the next stop sign, Ben had finished and withdrawn from the window, taking back his middle seat. Trish should have given him the other window seat. Instead of sitting next to me, she'd rather make us all suffer.

"Sorry, Maeve," Ben said.

"As long as you don't get any on me, I won't have to punch you," I said and patted his leg.

"Is there any vomit in my car?" the driver asked, again, eyeing me angrily in the rearview mirror.

"Not *in* your car," I said and peered out the open window at the grotesquely streaked exterior.

The driver wasn't interested in driving us into the apartment complex. He simply dropped us off on the street, then jumped out to survey the damage to his back door. "You owe me a carwash!" he yelled.

"Give me a break. That'll come right out with Windex and paper towels," I said. "I'll give you an extra tip for your trouble and still give you five stars, even though you're being an ass."

The guy huffed something under his breath and climbed back in the driver's seat.

I peered in and saw he was going straight for his phone. "And you better not dump my rating!" I yelled, slapping the driver's side window with my palm.

The driver flipped me off and sped away from

the curb. Luckily, he hadn't run over my feet. If he had, I would have totally sued his ass.

Ben was hunched over in the grass by the sidewalk, with Trish knelt beside him, her shoes dropped haphazardly on the sidewalk.

"Jesus, Ben. How much more do you have?" I said with a sigh.

"We don't need your sarcasm right now," Trish snapped.

"I'm fine," Ben said between coughs, then pushed back up to his feet. "I'm fine." Trish grabbed his arm to steady him, then bent down to grab her heels.

I let Trish handle Ben on her own until we got to the stairs, then I offered another hand while we climbed to the second floor. I unlocked the door and held it open so the others could enter, then stepped into the apartment living room and flipped on the lights.

It had been a long night and I was exhausted. All I wanted to do was trade these tight clothes for some comfortable pajamas and crash on the couch. I didn't even want to think about the fighting that would ensue tomorrow.

However, as soon as I turned toward the room after bolting the door, I saw it...

Ben and Trish headed toward the bedroom, and as they crossed the living room, they walked right through a gash of shimmering blue light hanging in the air. The ghostly light looked just like what I'd seen at the top of the lonely tower.

They passed right through the glowing, suspended cut like it wasn't even there.

"Ben. Trish. Stop," I warned, not wanting to venture any farther into the room. "We have to get out of here—*right now.*"

CHAPTER 3

"What are you talking about?" Trish asked, noticeably annoyed.

"Someone is in the apartment," I said, hoping that would scare her out of her irritation with me.

"How do you—" but her question trailed off at the sound of the toilet flushing. "Oh my God!" she whisper-screamed and tugged on Ben's arm to lead him back in the direction of the door.

"Is someone in the bathroom?' Ben asked.

"Someone's in the apartment," Trish said, pulling him back toward me.

"But *I* have to use the bathroom," Ben said, just as his foot snagged on the coffee table, sending him sprawling to the floor with an agonizing grunt. Trish was able to let go just in time to keep herself from collapsing too.

I ran to Ben and desperately tried to pull him to

his feet. Trish joined in the effort, but even with both of us, we needed him to help. We couldn't lift his dead weight, even with him being a relatively skinny guy.

Before we could get Ben back on his feet, a girl in a black hoodie and matching locks spilling out from either side of the hood ventured out of the bedroom. I blinked a few times to make sure I wasn't seeing Razielle. However, she wasn't my friend. I didn't recognize her, but from the way she immediately singled me out from the group, it seemed she recognized *me*.

"Come on!" I yelled, continuing to tug Ben awkwardly, which only resulted in him faceplanting back onto the carpet.

"No need for everyone to run off," the girl said, snapped her fingers, and Ben and Trish seemed to freeze in mid struggle.

I was still trying to pull Ben, and the effort sent me tumbling backward. But I certainly wasn't frozen... I seemed to still be in control of my body.

The girl strolled into the living room, looking calm—and rather amused. "I'm sorry about that. I've been waiting here for a while and I just couldn't hold it any longer." Then she tapped Trish on the top of the head, who then obediently came back to life, walked over to the couch, and sat down. Once seated, her body seemed to refreeze, her eyes wide, staring blankly across the room.

The girl tapped Ben next, and he proceeded to join his girlfriend on the couch, then also returning to an inanimate state.

I was still on the floor, inching toward the door, when the girl finally brought her attention back to me. "This can be quick and painless if you just cooperate," she said, offering a small smile.

"Who the hell are you?" I demanded.

"Quintiana, but my friends call me Quin."

"Do I look like one of your friends? And that still doesn't answer the question of *who* you are and why you broke into our apartment."

"I didn't break in," she said, sweetly.

"I'd say an otherworldly portal is just as bad as breaking down the front door."

Quin glanced behind her at the shining blue cut across the room, then back at me. "You can see the seam? I didn't think you were a seamstress anymore."

"And I suppose you are?"

Quin just laughed. "I wish. No; I've just trained myself to see the openings I make." Her hand went to the hilt of a dagger at her hip, which she then pulled out, flashing the blade.

"It's not as elegant as the needle, but it does the trick." Quin came closer to me with the dagger still out and I didn't know what she planned on using it for next. It seemed to be able to cut between worlds, and I was willing to bet it could cut flesh just as easily.

My eyes remained intently on the dagger as I scooted backward, until I hit the door.

Quin realized what I was staring at and laughed. "Oh, I'm not going to cut you," she said and sheathed her weapon.

"What do you want from me?" I asked, my heart pounding wildly in my chest.

Quin squatted beside me and removed a syringe from her hoodie pocket. "Now don't freak out," she said. "I just need some of your blood."

Don't freak out! Is she insane?

Hoping for the element of surprise, I batted at her hand holding the syringe as hard as I could, knocking it out of her grip. She was also unbalanced in her squatted position, so I kicked at her knees and sent her sprawling backward. Scrambling to my feet, I jumped on top of her, pinning both arms beneath my knees, then sending a fist straight toward her nose. I knew one would not be enough, so I punched her repeatedly, with the hope of finally knocking her out. If I was able to do that, then I hoped the spell Ben and Trish were under would break and we could successfully escape.

However, after several blows, I noticed Ben and Trish calmly standing up from the couch and approaching me. They still didn't look like themselves—obviously still under some sort of mind control. If I released Quin to protect myself, then she'd have time to recover and regain the upper hand. But if I didn't address the zombie versions of my friends coming at me, then I'd probably find myself in just as much trouble.

"Ben! Trish! Don't!" I pleaded, but it was no use. Their sense of reason was gone.

Ben grabbed one arm, Trish grabbed the other, and together they hauled me off Quin with ease. I tried to break free, but their grips were ironclad. Ben had no unsteadiness from his previous inebriation, and Trish's strength was incredibly impressive given her size.

"Let go of me!" I cried, but there was no empathy, emotion, or even humanity in their eyes.

Quin pushed up onto her elbows, then sat upright. Her face was bruised and bloodied, and she dabbed at the wet blood still leaking from her nose.

"I told you not to freak out," Quin said, painfully. Then she got to her feet and looked me square in the eyes. While I was securely held by my two room-mates, Quin balled up a fist and gave me a taste of my own medicine, punching me square in the nose.

The explosion of pain was immediate, as were the uncontrollable tears pouring down my cheeks. Then I was hit with the awful metallic taste of blood as it poured over my lips.

"Son of a bitch," I said as I tried to blink the tears away and regain some of my vision.

My legs grew weak and I wanted to collapse onto the floor, but my roommates held me up. Quin wiped her nose as she went to retrieve the syringe.

"Why are you doing this?" I cried, peppering the carpet around my feet in blood.

"I told you, I need some of your blood," Quin said. "That's it. Then I'll be on my way. Unless you want to make things more difficult."

I was good at making things *more* difficult. I guessed that could be considered another one of my superpowers.

"But why?" I asked. "Why do you need my blood? What's special about me?"

But to this question, she didn't provide an answer. Quin quickly grabbed my forearm, twisted, and jabbed the needle into my tender flesh. When she began to extract my blood, I had to look away. I was so done with needles. And before I knew it, she was finished and capping a small vial now filled with my blood.

"There. I think I've got what I need," Quin said, stuffing the vial into her pants pocket.

"Will you at least tell me how you found me?" I asked. I needed to know what I'd done that now put Ben in danger.

Quin stuffed a hand into her hoodie pocket and pulled out a torn envelope, dropping it onto the coffee table. To my frustration, I realized immediately that it was the envelope from Ben's latest letter.

I had tossed the empty envelope in the trashcan under Nym's desk, which wasn't something that filled quickly. We couldn't have emptied it more than once a month. Even though I hadn't planned on my sudden exit from Spellcrest Academy, I still cursed myself for being careless. I didn't know how she'd gotten the envelope and didn't want to believe that either of my roommates had sold me out. However, I needed to accept that as a very real possibility.

"How did you get that?" I seethed.

"It was given to me," Quin said, clearly unaffected by my anger.

"Who gave it to you?"

"You sure do ask a lot of questions, but I'm tired and now need to go fix my broken nose, so I'm not really in the mood to hang around and chat." Quin headed for the glistening gash in the center of the room. "I don't expect to see you again, so have a nice life," she said before stepping through the shimmering seam and disappearing into another world. I could only assume it was Kicryria and I knew chasing after her would be a big mistake.

As soon as Quin was gone, Ben and Trish dropped to the floor like they'd each been shot, taking me down with them. Trish's head banged against mine as we hit the floor, throwing me more into Ben. The three of us on the ground were a mess of tangled limbs.

My face still hurt like hell and now my head was aching from where Trish had head-butted me. It took much of my remaining strength to free myself from their dead weight. Both of them were out cold and for a moment, I actually thought they were dead. Then I noticed them breathing and slightly relaxed.

I gazed up at where Quin had escaped our world and saw the gash was still there, clear as day.

I crawled next to Ben and lightly slapped him in the face to get his attention. "Wake up, Ben!" I said, not knowing exactly what she'd done to him. "Wake up, damn you!"

I was about to grab some water from the kitchen when I noticed him stir. Trish made a sound a moment later.

Oh, thank God.

"What happened?" Ben groaned.

"Why are we on the floor?" Trish asked before I had a chance to respond.

"I don't know," I said, thinking fast. "I just woke up too. I was on the floor, the same as you."

"I don't remember falling."

"Maeve, what happened to your face?" Ben gasped.

I touched a hand to my upper lip and it came away wet with blood. "I—I must have hit my head when I fell," I said. "Damn, that hurts."

"Ben, are you okay?" Trish asked.

"I think so…" he said, though he didn't sound so sure. "When did we get home?"

"I don't know. I don't even remember the clock striking twelve."

"You don't?" I asked. "You don't remember taking an Uber home and Ben—" at seeing the confused looks on both their faces, I quickly stopped midsentence.

"What about Ben?" Trish asked.

"Nothing," I said. "I mean, he was just singing and getting the driver upset."

"Oh…" Trish glanced over at Ben, who was now climbing to his feet. "I'm so confused. What happened?"

"We must have had some bad appetizers," I said, though I knew it was a lousy explanation. But they were so out of it, they'd almost believe anything right now. "Happy freakin' New Year. Am I right?"

"I think I'm gonna go lie down," Ben said, stumbling in the direction of the bedroom—headed straight for the gash still visible to me in the center of the living room. He passed right through it without noticing it whatsoever.

"Do you want an ice pack or something?" Trish asked, now on her feet too.

"I'll wash myself up in the kitchen. I'll be fine," I said.

She nodded and followed Ben into the bedroom.

I walked over and dropped onto the couch,

feeling like my whole body had been put through a meat grinder. I was too drained to clean up all the blood. Hopefully, the stains would come out of the carpet, but I wasn't overly optimistic.

This had already been a long fucking night, but with that open seam in the middle of the room staring back at me, I knew it wasn't over yet.

CHAPTER 4

The apartment wouldn't be safe with an open portal to another world smack dab in the middle of it. Quin had left it open, and I wouldn't have known how to close it even if I'd still had my needle—which I didn't.

We couldn't continue to have people from Kicryria waltzing in and out of here like we were a freakin' bus stop. And since Quin and whoever she was working for had found me here, it didn't seem like this apartment would be safe for any of us going forward. Unfortunately, I didn't exactly know how to break the news to Ben.

At least I knew the first step I needed to take, even though I really didn't want to. I fished my phone out of my pocket and scrolled to Devon's number. I hadn't looked at it in weeks, but as angry as I was with him, I also hadn't been able to bring myself to delete it. Now, it would actually come in useful.

I pressed my thumb to his name to initiate the call, fully aware it was still the middle of the night—well, more early morning for him since he was an hour ahead. But I almost wasn't surprised to hear his groggy voice after four rings.

"Hello? Maeve, is that you?" Devon asked. I couldn't tell what he sounded like besides exhausted. But then again, I was also exhausted and wasn't in the best frame of mind to examine anything right now.

"Hey, Devon. Yeah; it's me," I said. "Sorry to bother you at this ungodly hour, but—"

"Happy New Year."

"Oh, yeah—Happy New Year to you too."

"Did you just get in from a night of partying?"

"Not exactly," I said. "I need your help—actually, your mom's help. But I don't have her number, so I'm calling you."

"You're calling me just to talk to my mother?" Now he sounded more confused than tired. Maybe there was some bitterness in his tone as well—it was hard to tell.

"There's an open seam or portal—or door to Kicryria or something—in the apartment where I'm staying," I said.

"There's a what?" Now he was awake.

"There was someone here, waiting for me when I got home…"

"Are you hurt? Where are you? Where did you go?" Devon fired off each question in rapid succession.

"I'm back in Hollywood, rooming with a friend."

"Does this friend have a name?"

I was reluctant to provide a name, but figured he'd find out anyway. "Ben," I said weakly.

Then the other side of the line went quiet. At first, I wasn't sure if Devon had hung up. Then his voice returned, detached like he'd been when I'd first met him in Lab. "I'll let the headmistress know right away, so she can sew it up. Give me the address."

I did as he asked, then Devon promptly hung up the phone. He made it loud and clear how much he *didn't* want to talk to me.

That's fine. It just makes things easier.

I had no idea how long it would take for the headmistress to arrive—someone else I really wasn't thrilled about seeing. It wasn't like Devon gave me any kind of estimated time, just that he'd *let her know.*

We are so gonna have to move.

I lay down on the couch, but never took my eyes off the blue light hanging in the air. A whole other world was just a few steps away. The vial of my blood was being used for something in that world, which I couldn't even imagine what. And Finley was probably in there somewhere, enjoying my powers with his troublesome new friends. A part of me wanted to go in there and slap the shit out of him, but I was terrified of stepping through that doorway without some type of lifeline. The headmistress had used enchanted chess pieces—which Devon had called totems—to help her get back to this world. I considered myself a relatively daring person, but at this point, I had to draw the line at stepping into alien worlds.

As exhausted as I was, I couldn't bring myself to close my eyes or look away from the open seam for a second. I didn't want to be taken by surprise by someone—or *something* else venturing into our living room. I made it a personal mission to stay on watch until the headmistress arrived, even if it took until sunup. Sleep would have to wait until tomorrow. Luckily, my aching face would also help keep me awake.

THE SUN WAS JUST STARTING to rise by the time someone knocked on the door, which was a hell of a lot better than someone else simply appearing in the middle of the room. Another appearance like that would probably have given me a heart attack.

I glanced in the direction of the bedroom before heading toward the front door. The bedroom door was still closed, and I didn't hear any sound coming from inside.

I opened the door to reveal the stern face of Headmistress Christi. She was in a high-collared long black dress with a glistening crystal sitting against her subtle chest. She obviously had an aversion to letting anyone see her octagram tattoo.

She shook her head at the sight of me. "You're a mess, child," she said.

"Thanks," was all I could think to say in reply, holding the door open for her to enter. "It's over there."

The headmistress strolled into the room, looking around as if assessing the place, then stepped up to the shimmering seam.

"I guess I shouldn't be surprised that you can still see it, given who your father was," she said.

"And who was he?" I asked, bitterly. "Were you ever going to tell me about them?"

"In time. There was no reason to bombard you with everything at once. You said someone came through?"

"Yes. A girl I'd never seen before. She said her name was Quin."

"The name doesn't ring a bell. Is she still in this world or did she go back?"

"She went back after taking a vial of my blood. Why would she want that?"

"You should have asked *her* the question," the headmistress said, nonchalantly.

"*I did.* She wouldn't tell me."

"Then your guess is as good as mine. Though I will admit it's strange."

"Thanks. That's super helpful."

The headmistress shrugged, then stepped into the seam, disappearing from the room.

"Headmistress Christi?" I said, afraid to be left alone in the room without an assurance she was coming back. I stepped up to the gash in the air and peered into the void. The shining edges cast shadows into the void and I couldn't see a goddamned thing. "Headmistress?" I called again, but there was still no answer. I had no idea if she could even hear me on the other side of the portal.

On shaking legs, I stepped closer to the seam, then reached a hand out. As the tips of my fingers touched the void, it felt a little like dipping my hand in a still lake of cool water. My hand didn't fully disappear, but it was no longer fully here, either. It appeared hazy and distorted, and I quickly pulled it back.

I examined my hand, which seemed fine apart from my bloody knuckles. I quickly convinced myself there was nothing to fear and the head-mistress was my lifeline for getting home. So I took the final step, ready to step through when Headmistress Christi appeared in the opening and pushed me away as she climbed back into the room.

"You should stay away from the seam," she said. "For your own safety."

"I didn't know if you were coming back," I said.

"Of course, I was coming back. But I first wanted to determine where it led."

"And?"

"And it leads to a suburb of the Kicryrian city of Ogginosh. I've explored that city before." The head-mistress pinched her forefinger, quickly exposing her needle. She pulled it out, with the thin red thread continuing to unspool from her finger.

"Did you see anyone there who'd attacked the Academy?"

"Since I wasn't at the Academy when it was under attack, then I don't know who all was there. However, I do know that we should not have lost our latest seamstress-in-training in that attack." She gave me a disapproving glare before stepping up to the seam and beginning to sew it up. Her needle went in and out of sight as she made small stitches, starting at the bottom edge of the diagonal and working upward. As she continued, the stitches disappeared along with the line where the seam had been, making the shimmering seam smaller with every stitch.

"I didn't plan on having my powers stolen from

me," I snapped. "But then again, I guess that was inevitable anyway, wasn't it?"

Headmistress Christi stopped stitching for a moment and turned her head toward me. "What are you insinuating?"

"You planned to steal my powers all along," I blurted out.

"And who would make you believe a silly thing like that?"

"Your son."

Her jaw tightened, much like Devon when he became angry. She looked like she wanted to rebuke me for such a brash statement, but instead, she turned back to what was left of the seam and continued her careful stitch work.

When she was done and the blue light had been fully extinguished, she finally addressed me again. "What you did was reckless and proved why you didn't deserve the honor in the first place. And because of your actions, you've put us all at even greater risk. We are now short a seamstress and it's not like I can just go and train another one. There are no more replacements. You left us shorthanded and vulnerable."

"I'm sorry," I said. "If I'd known more about my abilities and vulnerabilities, then this wouldn't have happened. And it still doesn't change the fact that my abilities were going to be taken from me anyway."

"I won't lie to you. You were *not* Helena's agreed-upon successor. I had no intention of allowing you to retain those coveted abilities long term. But they would still be here in the rightful hands of Earth's protectors. We would still have a seamstress—or tailor—to protect our borders."

"I know Devon was the chosen successor," I said. "So you don't have to keep beating around the bush."

"Devon might have spilled some insider information to you, but he wasn't privileged to everything. You have no idea what goes on behind the scenes to keep this world stable from magical influences and foreign invaders. It's true I wanted Devon to be the successor, but it didn't mean that's what actually was going to happen. There are people I report to as well. Compromises must be made for the greater good."

"Then who was it going to be?" I asked.

"I am not about to keep answering your questions," the headmistress shot back. "You are not in a position to demand answers to these types of questions. Now, if you'll excuse me, I still have *your* mess to clean up. And I would suggest you keep yourself out of trouble unless you want to be further dealt with."

As hurtful as many of the current events were, I didn't want to completely forget them all. I didn't want to have lost Finley with no memory of why. I didn't want to forget that magic existed in the world, and I didn't want to forget the few friends I kept in touch with. I wouldn't have minded erasing Devon, but knew I couldn't be so selective.

"No need to send a cleaning crew for me," I said. "I'll keep the secret of magic to myself."

"I wouldn't send a cleaning crew to wipe your memory," she said with a hard expression. "I'd send an extractor for your soul and wear you around my neck."

CHAPTER 5

I never took kindly to threats, but knew when I was outmatched. Headmistress Christi was *not* someone to screw with. I was starting to wonder who the true enemy was.

The headmistress marched out of the apartment with the threat still lingering in the stale air. Even with the seam gone, the apartment still felt vulnerable and exposed. I wasn't sure I liked having the headmistress knowing where I lived any more than the Kicryrians.

Shit. We really need to move.

Once I was alone again, I went to the kitchen to wash my face, which still hurt like hell. The headmistress hadn't offered to heal me, and I still had my pride, so I just had to tough it out. I grabbed a bag of frozen peas from the freezer; the bag was stiff from being in there for so long. This was one of several I'd bought months ago for Ben after an episode when he'd nearly cracked his head open. Now, it was my turn to get some use out of them.

Back in the living room, I rummaged through my bag for pajamas and finally slipped out of the previous night's tight clothes and into something infinitely more comfortable. Then I crashed onto the couch and placed the bag of peas across my face—icepack *and* sleep mask.

However, I couldn't have been lying down for more than five minutes when there was another knock on the door.

"Holy hell; what now?" I whined as I removed the peas from my face. I dropped the bag onto the coffee table and padded to the front door. When I peered into the peephole, I was surprised to find Devon standing on the second-floor landing.

I don't need this right now.

Just as he was about to knock on the door again, I threw it open. "What the hell are you doing here?" As I held the door, I barred the opening with my body.

After one look at me, his hard expression softened. "God, Maeve. What happened?"

Even though I'd washed away much of the blood, I knew my face was still a mess. "I told you—I was jumped by some Kicryrian girl. But don't worry, she didn't get away unscathed. I'm pretty positive I broke her nose."

"But she can probably also heal herself. You can't."

"Thanks for pointing that out. Did you come all this way just to point out the obvious?"

"*No*," Devon said in an irritated tone. "I came all this way to make sure you were okay."

"Well, as you can see, I am." I could be just as irritated with him. "So, have a nice trip home."

Devon's gaze dropped from my face, which was something I was used to since I was a girl and God had endowed me with boobs. Then it had become about the octagram tattoo on my chest. But now I realized it was because I was standing in the open doorway in my flannel pajamas, something he'd never seen me in before since our relationship at the Academy had been so secretive.

"This is ridiculous," Devon said. "Are you going to let me in?"

"Why?" I asked, defiantly.

"Because we haven't had a chance to talk since the night you left. I don't want to leave things that way."

"Well, whose fault is that?"

"Yours!" he exclaimed. "You wouldn't talk to me after it had happened, then you ran away from school the same night without telling anyone—or telling anyone where you were going. Your room-mates were the only ones who knew that you'd gone, but you hadn't even given them an address. I wanted to call you like a million times—"

"They had it, they just didn't know it," I said, thinking back to the black-haired girl who'd broken into the apartment just a few hours ago. She'd gotten the address from my dorm room—at least, someone had.

"They're worried about you."

"I talk to them all the time."

"Fine. *I'm* worried about you," Devon said.

"Are you sure? It's probably just residual feelings from the crystal." It didn't go unnoticed that he had a new one around his neck, though it was meant to be inconspicuous under his shirt.

"That's not fair. I didn't know about the crystals any more than you did. Are you saying you didn't have any feelings for me? Our initial pull toward each other may have been due to the crystals, but it doesn't mean that it didn't turn into something real —genuine feelings. If you truly feel nothing for me, then I'll leave you alone and never bother you again." He searched my wounded face for some sense of my true feelings.

That was when I finally stepped aside and allowed him to enter the apartment. I was still angry with him for not telling me about my parents, but I couldn't deny that having him at my apartment door now made me long to be in his arms again. But that wasn't something I would freely admit to him, at least not yet. If he truly wanted to get back into my good graces, he would have to work for it.

Devon paced the living room—otherwise known as my bedroom—while I closed and bolted the door. When I turned back to him, I found him gazing down at the coffee table—at the bag of peas and the ripped envelope.

"Why don't you sit down and let me heal you? You've got to be in pain."

"It's manageable," I said, but headed toward the couch just the same.

Devon sat beside me and coaxed me to lie down. *Make up your mind.*

I suddenly became very aware of how close he was to me and how much I'd wanted this back at the Academy. Devon grabbed the peas from the coffee table and gently placed them over my nose.

"I could do *that* myself," I said, sarcastically.

"Shut up, Rhodes. Now, just to warn you, I'm not the best at this. I can bring the swelling and inflammation down, but I don't think I can mend broken bones. *Is* your nose broken?"

"I don't know," I said and took a deep breath while waiting for him to perform his literal magic.

After a moment, I felt more pressure on the bag of peas like he'd placed his hand on it and was pushing down—not hard, but applying moderate pressure. At first, it hurt more than before, but the sharp pain began to steadily subside as a soothing coolness seeped into my skin.

It became so relaxing, I started to feel myself drifting off to sleep. But before slumber could fully take me away, Devon removed the peas from my eyes, letting in the growing morning light.

I blinked my eyes open and gazed into Devon's beautiful blue eyes.

"How's that?" he asked.

I carefully touched my face, ready to wince at a sharp pain, but didn't find an overly sensitive spot. My nose was still a little tender, but nothing like the pain it had been in before.

"I feel better," I said. "How do I look?"

"Beautiful," Devon said, making me smile.

Damn him.

"Why didn't you call?" I said, after pausing to gather my wits. I'd thought about this potential interaction for over a month now, turning it into a huge self-righteous fight—standing my ground, making brilliant and valid points, and kicking his ass out the door. But now, with him here before me, I felt none of those things. Now I simply felt sad, empty, and alone. And I could tell from the look in his eyes, all those heartbreaking emotions were weighing on him too. He had hurt me by not telling me about my parents earlier, and I had hurt him by running away into the night.

"I tried to," Devon finally said. "I wanted to. But

every time I looked at your name in my phone, I remembered how crushed you looked when I told you about your parents—that I was the one who'd made you look that way. I knew you were already having a hard time trusting me, and that admission pushed you over the edge. I hadn't expected you to leave that night, so I'd hoped for a chance at redemption. But you did... proving what you really wanted... to leave all of Spellcrest behind. To leave me."

"I didn't belong there anymore," I said. "It's exclusively for magicals and I'm not one anymore. I'm back to just being me. And what would you want with me anyway? Why would you settle for a Norm?"

"You're not a Norm to me. In fact, you're not a Norm at all," Devon said. He went to touch my leg, then pulled away, not sure if he was overstepping. "Didn't you learn anything in your classes? What are Norms?"

"Non-magicals."

"And what are non-magicals?"

"People that can't do magic," I said.

"People who don't know that magic exists—whose eyes haven't been opened. Yours have. You may not have your needle anymore, as well as many of the abilities seamstresses are endowed with, but you still have access to magic. It flows through you just like everyone else."

MICHAEL PIERCE

"I still have powers?" I asked, feeling the hope growing inside me.

"I believe you do," Devon said, giving me a warm smile.

"Who's this?" a voice asked from across the room.

My gaze shot over to the kitchen where Trish was standing in an oversized Coachella tee-shirt she often wore to bed, her red hair up in a messy bun. She almost looked... happy.

"My name's Devon. I'm a... friend of Maeve's," he said, rose, and crossed the room to shake her hand.

"It's a pleasure, Devon the mystery man," Trish said, her gaze returning to me with a smile spreading over her lips. "Why have we never heard of you before?"

"We only met each other recently," I said. "I ran into him at the club last night. Don't you remember?"

I could see the gears turning in her head. "I'm sorry. Last night is a little fuzzy," Trish said.

"I'll say," Devon said with a laugh. "It was a wild night."

I gave him a warning glare. *Do not go into detail.*

"What was a wild night?" Ben asked as he exited the bedroom. He was dressed in basketball shorts and an undershirt. Then he saw Devon and stopped in his tracks. "Who's this? Did he spend the night?"

"This is Maeve's new guy," Trish said.

"My friend," I clarified. "Ben, this is Devon."

46

They shook hands, but it clearly wasn't a friendly handshake. It was a challenge from the very start.

"And who are you?" Devon asked.

"An old friend of Maeve's," Ben said.

"Good. Then we're both friends of Maeve's."

"I guess so. Are you staying for breakfast?"

"No," I chimed in. "Devon was just leaving."

"I'd love to stay for breakfast," Devon said. "What are we having?"

"We don't really have much here," Trish said. "We'll probably have to go out."

"That's fine by me," Devon said. "Does that sound good to you, Maeve?"

"Why don't the three of you go and I'll go back to sleep. I get the feeling I'll be like a fourth wheel anyway." I turned onto my side and stretched out across the couch.

"Nonsense," Trish said. "It'll be a double date. Let me just go get some clothes on." Trish left for the bedroom and grabbed Ben's arm, but he shrugged her off.

"Yeah," Ben said. "Then you can tell us all about yourself. I'd love to know why we've never heard of you."

"Because I wanted to sidestep the integration," I said. "Seriously. You guys go. Bring me back a scone or something."

"If you want a scone, then you'll have to come

and order it for yourself." Ben disappeared into his room after Trish called for him several times.

"Then I don't want it that bad," I said, more to myself at this point.

"You should get dressed," Devon said, strolling back over to me.

"I'm seriously not going," I said. "And I'm not changing here in front of *you*."

"That wasn't what I was implying."

"You really need to go now. I can't handle any more arguing. Technically, last night is still going, and I need it to finally be over. I appreciate you coming here, but can you please go now? I can only ask nicely so many times before I go absolutely batshit crazy."

"Fine," Devon said. "But I want to see you again— under better circumstances. Will you think about what I said?"

"About coming back?"

Devon nodded.

"We'll talk about it more later," I finally conceded.

"Classes start in a week, so let's talk tomorrow."

I agreed and Devon patted my leg before heading for the door. I got to my feet and followed him, offering a hug before he ventured into the cold morning air. He squeezed me tight, his breath warm on my neck as we melted into the embrace.

When he released me, Devon looked deep into

my eyes and said, "Remember. You're not a Norm."
Then he was gone.

I closed the door and banged my head against it
for good measure. I was physically and emotionally
exhausted from everything that had happened over
the past twelve hours. If it was possible to be spiritu-
ally exhausted, then I was that too.

"Where's your guy?" Ben asked as he and Trish
exited their bedroom fully dressed.

"You scared him off," I said and returned to the
couch.

CHAPTER 6

I hadn't mentioned anything to Devon about me telling his mother that he'd spilled their secrets. First, that she was actually his mother. And second, that she'd intended to steal my needle for him to become a tailor. I didn't know what shit he'd get for any of that, so I had to prepare myself for some kind of backlash.

However, the subject didn't come up in our conversations over the next few days. And he was still talking to me, so that was a plus. I still didn't know what all this meant for us, especially with him at the Academy and me in Hollywood. Though he was supposed to graduate in two trimesters, so then other opportunities could open up. Maybe we could move to some other part of the country together. It could happen.

What I wouldn't give to still have magical

powers. I knew Devon said that I was still capable of magic, but every time I tried to do something within the realm of magic, I was given the cold reminder of what was possible in the real world. Everything I'd gained seemed to be gone.

Sitting on the couch, I repeatedly tried to balance a pen on my forefinger. I tried to picture it in my mind, steady and upright. It wasn't the most exciting thing, but I needed to start small. I'd remembered when Finley had done it—even removing his finger so the pen had remained suspended in the air, at least for a few moments.

I was simply waving my arm around trying to make it balance, which I couldn't even seem to do in a non-magical way.

"You must really be bored," Ben said, strolling out of the kitchen with a cup of coffee in one hand and a cigarette dangling from his lips.

What little concentration I had broke instantly and the pen dropped onto the floor. "Frustrated, not bored," I said.

"What are you frustrated about?" he asked, taking a seat beside me.

"You have a dream of becoming a fulltime DJ, and it's awesome," I started. "But I don't even have a dream. I don't know what I want to do. And I can tell I won't be welcome here much longer. So, I need to figure out something."

"You're welcome here as long as you need."

"But Trish—"

"Don't worry about Trish. I'll handle her."

I laughed, retrieving the pen from the floor. "Yeah, right. You still need to ask permission for what you're allowed to wear."

"Hey, now. Yes, I may give in easily for some of the smaller—less important—things. But when it comes to critical decisions, I'm in charge." He tapped his cigarette on the ashtray on the coffee table and took another inhale.

"*Okay*. You're the man of the house," I mocked, placing the pen back on my finger. "But the longer she's here, the more influence she'll get… and she's going to want this to be *your* space—as in the two of you, not three's company. And besides, it would be nice to have a bedroom again. Do you realize I haven't had my own bedroom since… since my first foster home? Every other home, I've shared a room with Finley."

"Until now," Ben said, finished his cigarette, then focused on his coffee. "He's got his own room now, right?"

"Yeah; I guess he does." I thought about all the homes we'd shared and all we'd been through together. I still couldn't understand how all of that led to him screwing me over for my powers.

"I remember having you guys right across the hall. That place wasn't so bad."

"It was one of the rare gems," I said. "Not entirely terrible."

"Wow; that's pretty impressive. You can always apply for the circus."

Ben was now focused intently on my hand, and when I looked down, I saw the pen perfectly balanced without me having to move my arm at all. I hadn't even noticed I'd finally done what I'd been struggling with for the past half hour. But with the sudden attention, I quickly lost control. Readjusting my arm couldn't even save it. I caught the pen as it toppled over.

"So much for that," I said with a sigh. Now that my balancing act had become the center of attention, I was done with that for the time being.

Ben usually played around with his DJ equipment while Trish was at work. So, once he finished his coffee, he set the mug in the sink and sat down at his workstation.

I began playing around with the pen again, but before I could get anywhere, my phone began to buzz on the coffee table, and I saw Razielle's name flash across the screen.

"You're still coming this weekend, right?" she asked, impatiently.

She'd asked me several times about me coming to her parents' house for the weekend before the start of the second trimester. I'd spent the last few weeks dodging the invitation, but after having seen Devon, it had made me miss them that much more, forcing me to finally give in.

"Yeah; yeah," I said. "I just secured the time off work. I owe several favors now, so you owe me."

"Awesome. Nym's flying out too. You wanted to leave from Burbank, right? I'll set you up with a charter plane for Friday morning. I'll text you the details."

When Friday morning rolled around, I had all my earthly possessions packed into the one suitcase I owned. I told Ben I'd see him in a few days and Trish nearly pushed me out the door. If I didn't know better, she'd have the locks changed by the time I got home. But I'd worry about my fragile living arrangements on Sunday. Today, I was just excited to be reunited with my magical freshman friends.

I took an Uber to the airport address Razielle texted me, which like the time we'd flown with Otis, wasn't by the main airport terminal. I was dropped off near a cluster of small buildings and hangars where I checked in, led to a small VIP lounge where I could partake in all the hors d'oeuvres and soda I wanted, then guided onto the tarmac with a small group of fellow travelers. The jet wasn't any bigger than the one I'd flown on previously, only this time I had to share the flight with a few business professionals, a family, and an energetic bachelorette party ready to rage in San Francisco. When the attendant wasn't looking, one of the girls offered me a glass of champagne, but I politely declined. For one, I didn't drink. And two, it was ten in the freakin' morning.

"You in college up there?" the girl with the tiara asked.

"No; just visiting some friends," I said.

"This is the only way to fly," one of the other girls said, and they collectively clinked glasses.

We flew into San Francisco Airport and I wished the bachelorette party girls a fun weekend. I hadn't spoken with anyone else on the flight. As soon as I descended the stairs with my bag, I saw Razielle and Nym standing at the edge of the tarmac. The pair of them smiled and waved, and I could feel myself instantly beaming as well.

As I walked toward them, the bachelorette party was right behind me and realized who I was meeting.

"Have fun, girls! Don't do anything we wouldn't do!" one of them exclaimed.

Razielle waved them off and Nym frowned in confusion. But once I reached them, everything else was forgotten. I hugged each of them.

"Welcome to The City," Razielle said, then eyed my rolling suitcase. "Don't you have a weekend bag or something? Are you like moving in? Not that I would mind."

"I don't have a weekend bag—or an overnight bag. This is all I've got. We've been on many adventures together. She hasn't let me down yet."

"It's a nice bag," Nym said. She was still afraid of my feelings being hurt. That was practically never the case, but I loved her for it anyway.

"I'm just so excited you're here," Razielle said, starting to walk toward the parking lot. "I wish I could've gotten you out here sooner. *I tried.*"

"*I know.*"

"I can't believe how quickly the holiday break has flown by."

I didn't know how we were getting back to her parents' house because I didn't think Razielle had her license yet, but once we reached the parking lot, I quickly realized we were headed straight for a black limousine.

Holy shit.

"You went all out," I said as the driver took my bag and the three of us piled into the roomy back seats.

"No," Razielle admitted. "This is just how my family operates. You kinda get used to it. Want a root beer?"

"You know me too well," I said with a smile.

"I can't take all the credit. Nym reminded me."

"Well, you're both amazing," I said.

Razielle handed me a root beer poured into a fancy glass of ice like the soda can wasn't good enough. In fact, I didn't feel good enough sitting on these leather seats.

"First time in a limo?" Nym asked.

"How can you tell?" I laughed and took a sip from my glass. The bubbles tickled my still healing nose. It even tasted better than drinking out of a can.

As we drove, I learned Razielle lived in Presidio Heights, just west of downtown. But just like LA, even though the drive wasn't far, it still took over a half hour to get there. Once we reached her neighborhood, I swore we were driving through Beverly Hills. The mansions were surreal. And hers was no little shack in a fancy neighborhood. We drove into a gated driveaway with a luscious landscape, larger-than-life stone fountains, and an elegant estate with giant pillars lining the front.

Nym was always polite and gracious, but she didn't look impressed. Her life was probably just as luxurious on the opposite side of the country. But this lifestyle was on an altogether different level to me. This was the kind of out-of-reach shit I read about in magazines.

"Don't worry," Razielle said. "My parents won't be all up in our business. And only one of my older brothers is actually around right now. Arius. He graduated last year and is still trying to figure out what he wants to do."

"From Spellcrest?" I asked.

"Yeah," Razielle said. "He might be here, but he shouldn't bother us too much."

"I'm sure he won't be a bother." He was closer to my age than either of these two, and I couldn't say

that I'd known an angel about my age before
—Nephilim.

What I hadn't expected and why her family
wouldn't be in our way was because Razielle
arranged for us to stay in the guest house around the
back of the property. It was a full-sized house with a
kitchen, living room, and three bedrooms. Forget
the mansion, I wouldn't mind living *here* forever.

Razielle showed us to our rooms. She planned to
take the third—roughing it in the guesthouse
with us.

My room had a queen-sized bed with a floral
comforter and matching curtains. The wood furniture matched as well and black-and-white city
photos hung on the wall. I even had my own
television.

"Is it okay?" Razielle asked as I dropped onto the
bed and stared at the far wall of framed pictures.

"Do you realize, I've never had my own room
before?" I said.

"I'd never shared a room until this year at the
Academy," Razielle said. "It was tough at the
beginning."

"Yeah; you were like a spoiled brat," I said. "And I
mean that in the nicest possible way."

"I know." She sat beside me. "I still am. I think
you're just used to it now."

"That's probably true," I said with a laugh.

"It hasn't been the same without you. I still hate you for leaving."

"I'm not a freakin' supernatural like you and the elven princess in the next room. My needle was stolen from me along with everything else."

"You're *so* dramatic," Razielle sighed and fell backward onto the bed. "Everyone's got magic—just most people don't know it. It's like you weren't even listening in class."

"I listen. It's just hard to believe, especially since there are supernaturals like you, and I was given something with specific power. It's hard to believe that the rest of us common folk have similar dormant abilities. The real world is not magical. Ask anyone."

"And that's why it remains non-magical. Your abilities are only dormant because of *you*."

"Look at you, sounding all old and wise," I said, falling back to lie beside her.

"I have my moments." Razielle laughed and rolled off the bed. "I should check on Nym. It's too quiet in the next room."

"She's always quiet."

"Which always scares me."

CHAPTER 7

"*R*ise and dine, sunshine," chirped a cheerful voice in the darkness.

I opened my eyes half expecting to see Nym and found myself nearly face to face with a little blond girl who couldn't have been any older than ten. Once she saw that I was awake, she left my bedside and threw open the curtains, allowing the morning sunlight to pour into my own private bedroom—mine, except for this strange little girl who'd woken me up from one of the most peaceful slumbers of my life.

"Who are you?" I asked, wiping sleep from my eyes.

"Elora," the girl said, sweetly—like that explained everything. "Breakfast is ready, so if you want it before it gets cold, then it's time to rise."

"And dine—I get it," I said, groggily. This was the

first night I'd had in a while sleeping in an actual bed. And this bed—this heavenly mattress—was unlike anything I'd ever experienced before. It seriously made every other mattress I'd slept on feel like a stone slab.

As I sat up in bed, Elora handed me a glass of water from the nightstand, which she must have also brought into the room.

"Hydration is important first thing in the morning," she said.

She didn't sound like a ten-year-old. And when I took a closer look at her, I noticed gossamer butterfly-like wings on her back—so delicate they were nearly transparent. So, she wasn't a typical tween after all.

"Thanks," I said and took a sip just as Elora disappeared before my eyes without saying another word.

What the hell?

As nice as the girl seemed, ghostly children creeped me out.

I nervously glanced around the room. The door was still closed. No one else was in the room with me—at least that I could see. Now that I was listening more closely, I could make out Razielle's and Nym's voices coming from outside.

I was now fully awake and left with my water to join the girls in the kitchen. Luckily, Elora was there too, so I didn't have to try and explain some delusion.

"I thought *I* was the late sleeper," Razielle said with a laugh. Both girls were fully dressed already.

"It wasn't my fault," I said, taking a seat at the table with the other two girls. "The bed was too damn comfortable."

"Did Elora scare you?" Nym asked, a small smirk spreading over her lips. "I'm assuming you're not used to fairies either."

"She's a fairy?" I gasped, but it was far better than the apparition I was fearing. "Elora, why didn't you tell me?"

"I just assumed you knew," she said, carrying a plate piled high with waffles to the table.

"You don't need to serve me," I said as she dropped two waffles onto the plate in front of me.

"It's part of her job," Razielle said. "She works here."

"Doesn't that break, like, child labor laws or something?"

"She's not as young as she looks. She's actually thirty-four."

"Wow," I said. "You look damn good for thirty-four."

"Thank you," Elora said. Her cheeks blushed a little, reminding me of Nym.

"Fairies aren't from Earth. She's here on... well, basically a work visa," Razielle said. "She's working toward her citizenship. It's a five-year process. And it's harder for most fairies since they look so young and childlike."

"The Valentines have been very nice to me," Elora said. "I'm thankful for all they've done. Would you like coffee?"

I guessed at this point it would be considered insulting not to let her do her job, so I simply said, "Yes, please."

WE HUNG out by the pool for most of the morning, even though it was too cold to go swimming. Instead, we talked about our winter breaks and some of what I'd missed after leaving the Academy last trimester.

Razielle's mother walked out from the main estate to introduce herself sometime before lunch. She was a tall, black-haired beauty, making it obvious where Razielle got her looks from. But unlike Razielle, her mother was dressed much more traditionally in light colors and natural makeup tones. I knew she was human—the human half of Razielle—but she had an overwhelming angelic air about her.

It seemed that Razielle's full angel of a father—incidentally also named Raziel and pronounced the same—was currently out of town on business.

As the three of us girls talked, I finally spilled the beans about the girl that had attacked me at the apartment, me requesting the headmistress, and Devon showing up at my doorstep.

"That's so weird," Razielle said.

"What do you think she wants with your blood?" Nym asked.

"I dunno. You know more about this magic stuff than I do," I said. "What kinds of things would someone's blood be used for? Would it be used for a spell or something?"

"There *is* blood magic," Razielle said. "But that's not something taught at the Academy. It's dark magic. It could maybe be used to track you."

"Or control your body," Nym offered.

I shuddered at the thought. "Neither of those things sounds good, but especially not the second one. And the last thing I want to become is a sleeper agent. For what purpose? It's not like I'm special anymore."

"To aid the Kicryrians in the war," Razielle said.

"I've never heard of them using that tactic, but I've heard of it being done before," Nym said.

"There's got to be some kind of protective spell against something like that, right?" I asked.

Razielle shrugged.

"There are," Nym said.

"It may be used to clone you," Razielle burst out.

"Holy shit! Is that possible too?" I asked, exasperated.

"Probably."

"Okay; I don't like where this discussion is going," I said. "I'm not gonna be able to sleep with these possibilities tormenting me."

"There's really only one thing to do," Razielle offered.

"Oh, yeah? And what's that?" I asked.

"Come back to Spellcrest."

Nym emphatically agreed—well, in her own reserved way. "That's the safest thing for you."

"Can't your family help with giving me a protective spell to keep me from going crazy and killing someone?" I asked.

"My dad could, but he probably won't be back before we leave for school. And the Academy is like a total safe haven. There's the protective barrier around the entire school and I know the professors would aid in protecting you. Professor Windsor for sure. What have you got to lose?"

"I don't see the headmistress letting me back in. She's not exactly my biggest fan," I said. *In fact, I totally freaking hate her.*

"Devon will talk to her—I know he will. You deserve to be there as much as anyone else. And we'll help you to get back to some of the abilities you had before."

Nym nodded. "All of us will help you—Ivanic, Erik, Sarah, Bree. Probably even Grayson, if you asked."

"I'd be going in there feeling like the biggest loser

in the school," I said, and thought back to my discussions with Finley and how inadequate he'd felt. If I did this, then I'd be following in his footsteps.

"Your brother had felt like he didn't have enough magic, either. Isn't that right?" Razielle asked, as if she was reading my mind.

"Yeah," I said. "It was our biggest source of tension."

"Well, there's also another reason to go back," Razielle began and leaned in closer. "Arius told me about a dagger that can be used to cut between worlds. If we can get our hands on it, we can go look for your brother. You want to find him, right? And get your needle back?"

Of course, I wanted that—though I didn't know to what end. I had to know what really happened. Had he really betrayed me or was he also a victim somehow? Either way, I still felt obligated to smack him upside the head. And I *would* take my needle back.

Then I thought about the dagger that girl who'd broken into the apartment had been carrying, wondering if it was the same thing. I hadn't specifically told that detail to Razielle and Nym. Now I was extra curious.

"I'm listening," I said.

"After I mentioned the stuff that happened with your brother, Arius told me about a Seam Dagger one of the Master Classmen professors has. He shows the class how a seam is opened, though they don't open one to another world—just one to the not-so-distant past. But Arius says it works for other worlds too; you'd just need a totem from that world to reach it. So, we'd just have to find one from Kicryria."

Totem. There was that word again. Devon had talked about them when he'd taken me to the headmistress's office. A totem provided an anchor or trail of breadcrumbs to get back to its world or time of origin. And the headmistress had hundreds of them from her extensive travels—her enchanted chess pieces.

"I know where one is," I said, feeling a smile creep over my lips as things appeared to be coming together.

"Where?" Razielle asked, her face lighting up.

"The headmistress has a collection of them—all labeled—and Devon had shown me one from Kicryria. And I'm sure she has more since I'm assuming that's a popular destination."

"I don't like the sound of this," Nym said, crossing her arms.

"We said we'd help our friend," Razielle said. "You can back out if you want, but I'm not." Then she turned her attention back to me. "And I still haven't forgiven you for ditching me in the teachers' lounge."

"I don't know what you're talking about," I lied. "I tried to pull you through, but we got separated."

"Yeah, right," Razielle said. "I know what you did, and it was noble of you, but don't shut me out again. We're in this together."

Hearing her say those words made my heart ache for Finley.

"I'm still in," Nym said.

"Then what do you say, Maeve? Are you coming back to Spellcrest?" Razielle asked expectantly.

"I suppose I am," I said, thinking of how much harder it would be the second time around—with *me* now being the magical dud. But I believed I could make enough progress to keep up in my classes while we continued to develop a plan to find Finley. One way or another, I was bringing him home. "I'll give Devon the good news, so he can make whatever arrangements are necessary. And damn, it's gonna be cold!"

CHAPTER 8

*T*here was something satisfying, as well as terrifying, with the thought of going back to Spellcrest. I called Devon that night to give him my final decision. He said he'd make sure my student status had remained active and I was still enrolled in all my classes. Devon wanted to make arrangements to fly me back on Sunday, but I told him I'd already be hitching a ride with Razielle and Nym. The harder call would be to Ben, breaking the news that I wasn't coming home—that I'd made up with Finley and would be going back to Riverside. Though I couldn't imagine Trish being too heartbroken over the news.

I also felt bad about the Jeep I wouldn't be returning to the rental lot twenty miles outside of Spellcrest, but I just couldn't imagine flying home and driving all the way out to Colorado when I could be relaxing on a private jet straight to Spellcrest.

ON SATURDAY, Razielle took us into San Francisco where we walked through Chinatown and Fisherman's Wharf. We took pictures at the Golden Gate Bridge and rode the boat to Alcatraz. Then it was back to her parents' mansion for dinner with her mother and older brother, Arius.

"So, this is the girl who had once been a seamstress," Arius said after we'd been introduced. He had rather intoxicating green eyes and short dark hair, though it wasn't black like that of the girls in his family. He had angular and rugged features, though the visible dimples when he smiled softened his expression—a smile that showed off perfectly white teeth. "That sounded like a tough break."

"Not my best day," I said, sarcastically. "But I'm determined to move forward."

"I like your gumption, kid," he said, patronizing me like I wasn't merely a year younger than him. I couldn't seem to get away from everyone treating me like I was a freakin' freshman.

"That's good because I was really looking for your approval," I said, rolling my eyes and turning to Razielle.

"Lay off, idiot," Razielle said and made sure she

put space between her brother and me at the dinner table.

Throughout the meal, I could feel his emerald eyes on me, but I did what I could to ignore the blatant attention. Luckily, he wasn't close enough to try footsies with me under the table.

"You girls looking forward to getting back to school?" Razielle's mother asked, then took a final bite of her salad before Elora cleared it from the table.

"It sure beats regular school," Razielle said.

"I really like it there," Nym agreed.

Then all eyes were on me. "I'm ready to give this magic thing another try," I said. "Hopefully, Combative Casting won't kick my ass too much. Sorry—I didn't mean..."

But before I could fully apologize, Razielle's mother simply laughed off my comment. "I didn't have the opportunity to go to Spellcrest when I was a teenager, but I've heard enough stories from Ictus, Arius, and now my baby girl."

"*Mom*, stop," Razielle whined, reminding me of her true age.

After dinner, we went back to the guest house to get comfortable and enjoy the evening. I threw on some pajama pants and ventured into the living room where Razielle was scrolling through endless titles on Netflix to find something to watch. Nym sat on the far side of the couch, noticeably turned off by everything Razielle chose. And just to be difficult, Razielle nixed every suggestion Nym made.

"How did you guys not kill each other while I was gone?" I asked, laughing as I plopped down between them.

"We get along," Razielle said, rather defensively.

"Yeah; it shows. No… we're not watching that," I protested when she stopped on another b-horror movie. "I've got enough nightmares in my head right now of what the Kicryrians may be planning to do to me."

"You'll be safe and sound back at the Academy tomorrow," Razielle said. "You'll see."

"Until we go after them on their home planet. I doubt my protection will extend that far."

"We'll just have to bring some protection of our own."

"Oh, that's a sweet movie," Nym interjected as Razielle continued to scroll.

"I don't want a *sweet* movie!" Razielle argued.

"It's two against one," I said. "*Pretty in Pink* it is," I said, trying not to sound too smug.

"Pretty nauseating is more like it." But Razielle relented and hit the start button.

DESPITE THE ANXIETY of going back and what the Kicryrians were doing with my blood, I was still able to sleep like a baby on the cloud of a bed in my own private room—well, private until Elora awoke me the following morning.

She fluttered around the room like a cheerful child, forcing me to stuff my head under my pillow when she threw open the curtains.

"This should *not* be part of your job description," I protested from under the pillow.

"It's not, but Miss Razielle instructed I get you up," Elora said, handed me a glass of water, and vanished from my bedside.

I felt surprisingly rested, though I still didn't want to get up. Perhaps I could replace the dorm mattress with this one. It would have to be cut in half, but it could work.

When I exited my room, the other bedroom doors were still closed. I ventured down the hallway to the main living area and found Elora cooking breakfast, which smelled incredibly delicious. But I couldn't help but notice she was alone.

"Where are the others?" I asked.

"Still sleeping," Elora said, nonchalantly, and kept right on working, her delicate wings flapping as she hummed to herself.

That minx. Two can play at this game.

I marched back into the hallway and barged into Razielle's dark room. She seemed to still be fast asleep. I marched straight for the window and threw open the curtains.

"Rise and dine, sunshine!" I barked like a drill sergeant, determined to get her attention.

Razielle jumped, her eyes shooting open at the sudden intrusion. When she realized it was me, a guilty expression flashed across her face. Then she groaned and stuck her head under her pillow.

"How do you like it?" I asked, snatching away her shield and tossing it on the floor. Unfortunately, there were multiple pillows on her bed, so she simply grabbed another one and buried her head under it.

"You're the devil," Razielle whined.

"So I've been told," I said and laughed as I grabbed the next pillow from her.

We went through this several more times, and when she was finally out of pillows, Razielle released her ivory wings and cocooned her body with them.

"Hey, that's not fair!" I exclaimed, both of us laughing by this time. "I can't pull them—" I started but stopped myself upon feeling the full weight of what I was about to say. Pulling the wings off an angel was no joke, especially after seeing the horror firsthand. My laughter quickly died.

Razielle peeked out through her feathers. "What's up?"

I shook my head, still picturing the ethereal appendages plucked from the angel warriors' bodies —hearing them scream and seeing the blood as it pooled on the stone floor.

"Don't worry about the Kicryrians," she said. "We'll be back on campus this afternoon. Nothing will happen to you."

"I know," I said, my voice sounding weak now. I hadn't told her what had been done to those angels. I didn't know if I'd ever be able to. "I think breakfast is almost ready." I needed to get some air, so I abruptly left the room.

Elora had awoken Nym by the time I returned to the kitchen, and we were all served once Razielle stumbled out of her room.

No one had much to pack. I had all my earthly belongings in the one suitcase, but I'd been pretty much living out of it all weekend, so I was ready to go in five minutes. The other two girls had only brought small overnight bags when they'd left for Christmas vacation since most of their stuff remained in the dorm room. They took slightly longer to pack their small bags, but we were all ready well before having to leave for our scheduled flight.

Again, we took the limousine to San Francisco Airport, but this time, we had a private jet for the three of us. As soon as we were greeted by the pilot, I realized I'd met him before—he was the guy who'd helped me escape Spellcrest on the night I'd lost my powers—not lost them, but had them stolen from me.

"How's your mother doing?" he asked, taking my bag since it was the biggest and bulkiest.

"What?" I asked, not expecting the question.

"Hadn't you said she was in the hospital? That's why—"

"Yes; I *did* say that," I said, now recalling our conversation, my excuse for having to leave so suddenly. "She's home now and recovering well."

"I'm glad to hear it," he said, ascending the stairs with my bag.

"Did he fly you the first time too?" Razielle asked, dropping the handle of her bag and carrying it up the stairs after the pilot.

I let Nym go next, then followed them into the jet. "No; that was the recruiter who'd betrayed the school. You remember him—right, Nym? Otis?"

"He seemed so nice," Nym answered, handing her bag to the pilot once he was done stowing the other two.

"So did her brother," Razielle added, dropping into one of the plush leather seats.

"Let's not dampen the mood by bringing up my brother," I said, taking the seat across from her. Nym then sat beside me.

There didn't seem to be anything magical about our takeoff until we were flying high over California. The rumbling and din of the engines steadily disappeared until the flight was smooth and silent. Soft music played from the overhead speakers like we were relaxing in some luxury spa—not that I'd actually been to a luxury spa before, but I'd seen them in movies and they were always portrayed the same.

The pilot came back and checked on us several times throughout the flight. He provided us with drinks and snacks, as well as pre-made sandwiches for an early dinner, which were still nothing to balk at.

The sky was purple with the sun sinking behind the mountains by the time we landed at the single-runway Spellcrest Airport. I threw on my leather jacket and gloves, doing what I could to prepare myself for the bitter cold I was no longer protected from.

And when I descended the stairs to the tarmac, I quickly noticed Devon's smiling face as he stood beside an SUV near the hangar.

"It seems the two of you have kissed and made up," Razielle said, elbowing me in the ribs.

"Somewhat," I said and waited for the pilot to carry down my heavy bag.

"There better be room in there for all of us," she yelled, walking in the direction of the SUV with her luggage in tow.

"No; the rest of you can wait for the next taxi," Devon said, trying to make it sound serious, but the corners of his lips continued to twitch.

"*Ha ha.*"

Nym hung back with me. It made me feel better that someone else was also shivering from the cold and biting wind.

"I don't suppose you ever returned the Jeep," the pilot said as he set my bag on the ground.

"I did not," I said, sheepishly. "But I promise I will —though I probably won't have time until spring break."

"Do you have the keys? I could have someone pick it up."

The guilt just intensified. "I—I don't," I said through chattering teeth. "But I can tell my room-mate to leave them out or give them to whomever you send."

"Don't worry about it," the pilot said. "Spring break will be fine. I'll just keep it off the books until then."

"Is that lot yours?"

"Of course. Why would you think I'd be okay with taking keys after hours?"

"I... umm... I just thought you were..."

"Stealing? I'm not a thief. I was just trying to help a girl in need."

Now I felt even worse for thinking so little of him. "I'm sorry. I shouldn't have assumed."

"Good luck on your next trimester," he said with a small smile before heading back into the jet.

Nym and I hurried to join Razielle at the SUV. The tarmac was clear, but there was snow piled high at the edges. The evening air was clear, with glistening diamonds shining overhead. But it was so cold it was heard to breathe, with thick clouds being expelled from my lungs like angry demons.

Devon took our bags one at a time and arranged them in the trunk of the SUV. He greeted the other girls, then stopped before me, gazing deeply into my eyes—seemingly conflicted about whether or not to welcome me with a kiss. Ultimately, his lips curled up into a sad smile, then he walked me to the passenger side with a hand at the small of my back and opened the door.

Razielle and Nym climbed into the back seat, and as soon as everyone was buckled in, Devon started to drive toward Spellcrest Village.

Everything was as I remembered it, looking like a quaint European town hidden away in the mountains. There were a few cars on the road, but mostly residents were walking around the downtown area with heavy coats and hoods.

And soon, the large stone wall of Spellcrest Academy loomed in the distance. The very top of the steeply-angled roof of the Manor peeked over the wall. The lonely stone tower was farther still, bisecting the night sky like a monument to the angels who'd lost their lives. I almost expected to see a light at the top, beckoning us back to finish the battle that had taken place there. But it was as dark and empty as a stone tomb.

Devon was quiet for most of the drive, leaving Razielle to do all the talking since she couldn't handle silence for more than a few seconds at a time.

I gazed out the side window at the winter wonderland of a campus. The topiaries that decorated the grounds were covered in snow like everything else, though some of what had accumulated was now piled around their bases from the constant wind.

It didn't take long before Devon pulled into the roundabout for Windsor Hall. He stopped before the main entrance and shut off the engine.

"Home sweet home," he said, offered a smile— again more on the sad side—then hopped down to retrieve our bags from the trunk.

He tried to take mine, but I grabbed the handle from him. "I can do it. I may be less magical, but I'm not helpless."

"I'd never even insinuate that," he said and pushed the clicker to lock the doors. It wasn't until we got inside and stepped into the open lobby, that Devon stopped us and finally broke the news. "Maeve, let me show you to your new room."

"I haven't been gone that long," I said, sarcastically. "I think I remember where it is—we all do."

"Umm... Maeve, you're no longer rooming with them."

I shot Devon an incredulous look. "You're kidding, right?"

CHAPTER 9

"*I*'m afraid not," Devon said, and the seriousness of his expression told me he wasn't lying. "But this doesn't have to be a bad thing."

"How can it not be a bad thing?" I scoffed, glancing over at Razielle and Nym, who were both as dumbstruck as I was. "We had a great arrangement and we're practically sisters now. I don't want to start over with someone else. I've bounced around too many times. I'm not putting up with any shit from some new neophyte."

"You won't have to," Devon said, his tone soft. "Let me just show you to your room."

I glared daggers at him, but I ultimately knew this wasn't his doing. After taking a deep breath, I finally allowed myself to calm down and turned to my ex-roommates. "I'll come see you in a little bit and tell you all about how screwed up my new living situation is."

"Okay," Razielle said. "You know where to find us."

I gave them each a hug, feeling like we were leaving each other for good—again—then let them head upstairs as I followed Devon past the stairs.

"Where are we going? I thought this was the boys' wing," I said.

"Well, this boys' wing just got its first girl," Devon said, not sounding overly enthused about the whole idea.

"If you think I'm going to room with some random boy, then you're sadly mistaken."

"You're making it sound like I orchestrated this. I had nothing to do with it. But, don't worry—that's not the arrangement." Then Devon stopped. "Here we are."

I looked at the number on the door we stood before and realized precisely where we were.

"I'm not rooming with Grayson either," I protested. We were stationed at his and Finley's door.

"Again, that's *not* the arrangement," Devon said, produced a key from his pants pocket, and opened the door. He held it open and gestured for me to enter.

As I crossed the threshold, I saw the truth of my new living situation. The room had been cleared of everything but the school-issued furniture. What had once been Finley's bed had his packed suitcase sitting atop it, waiting to be claimed by his last remaining family member. On Grayson's side, even the sheets for the bed were folded in a neat pile.

"What happened to Grayson?" I asked, turning back to Devon.

"He left for the holidays, then his parents contacted the Academy and pulled him out due to everything that had happened," Devon said. "He was severely shaken."

"Though he came through in the end. He was a good kid." My eyes wandered back to Finley's luggage. "I'm surprised this is still here."

"The professors checked your brother's belongings in case there was anything significant he left behind," Devon said.

"And did they find anything?" I asked.

Devon shook his head. "But they still saved his stuff in case he came back for something. Though it doesn't seem like that's going to happen at this point."

I rolled my bag over to what had once been Grayson's desk and set it against the wall. "What you're saying, is that I have my own room," I said, turning back to Devon.

He remained by the door, almost as if he was afraid to enter the room. "I know that's a rarity where you come from, and I hope the change isn't too terrible."

"I think I can get used to this." It had been so nice for the past weekend having my own room—my own space to retreat to when everything felt over-whelming. Of course, this bed wouldn't compare to the one I'd slept in for the past two nights, but I couldn't complain too much about that.

"And now I can say I've seen the inside of your room." Devon finally allowed for a small smile, reminding me of the boy I'd become so fond of before everything went to shit.

"And there's even an extra bed for you," I said, returning a sly smirk.

Devon glanced over at Finley's bed, then at his packed suitcase. "I've already lived in the neophyte dorm, so you won't catch me raising my hand to move back in."

"*Ouch*," I said, feigning offense. "Not even for the object of your desire?"

"I won't *object* to the occasional sleepover, but I'm not moving in."

"You make it sound so platonic." I forced a pout.

But before I could bait him too much, Devon strolled into the room, finally allowing the door to shut behind him. He closed the space between us, took my face in his hands, and pressed his full lips to mine. I no longer had a crystal to manipulate my emotions, but I still felt my body go weak just from the sensual way he touched me. I leaned into him, pressing my body against his, as we continued to explore our desires. All was not forgiven, but my body still reacted to him with uncontrollable want, so it couldn't all have stemmed from a mere necklace. He set my body ablaze as his hands traveled down the length of it and settled firmly on my hips, deepening our connection even more.

When our lips finally parted, I was tempted to ask him to stay. The bed I'd be claiming for myself may not have had the bed sheets on the mattress, but Finley's old bed was fully made and we could easily move across the room. However, before I had a chance to ask, Devon crushed the thought.

"I should let you get settled in," he said, taking a step back from me. "I have a few more things to take care of before the winter trimester begins. I'll see you tomorrow?"

I nodded, momentarily tongue-tied. *Get your shit together, Rhodes.*

"Yeah. It's been a long day anyway. 8 a.m. Morality of Magic will be here way too soon," I said, trying to mask my disappointment.

Devon leaned in to give me one more quick kiss, then pulled something from his pocket and forced it into my palm. "I secured this for you."

I gazed down at his gift to find it was another crystal necklace, shining in my hand like a tiny blue sun. "Is this…?"

MICHAEL PIERCE

"No—nobody we know. I made sure of that. And since we lost all the Kicryrian crystals, you don't have to worry about it being one of them either. It's simply the soul of a voluntary donor."

"What's the name?" I insisted. I didn't want to take any chances.

"Eileen something-or-other. I can't remember her last name. Do you know any Eileens?"

"No."

"Then I think we're in the clear." Devon returned to the door. "I'm glad you're back, Maeve." He finally gave me a full-sized genuine smile as he pulled the door open, then disappeared into the hallway, leaving me with an aching heart and a serious curiosity of my new *soulmate*.

I guess there are two girls in the boys' wing now.

CHAPTER 10

When I awoke the next morning, the first thing my eyes landed on was Finley's suitcase. The physical reminder of him was much harder than the mere thoughts of him before. I so wanted answers, which was one of the reasons I'd come back to the Academy—not just for me, but for him.

It also felt weird waking up in a bedroom alone even though I'd done it for the past two mornings. I half expected Elora to suddenly appear. When she didn't, and I fully wiped the sleep from my eyes, I was able to finally accept I was back at Spellcrest and a new trimester was starting.

I'd thought last trimester was an adventure, but with everything that had happened over the past month, I was venturing just as much into unknown territory. And with my severely decreased abilities, I wasn't sure I was ready for it—even with my new crystal, my mysterious passenger.

It would have been nice to have gotten a heads-up regarding the bathroom situation, even though I probably should have expected it. Since this was the first-floor boys' wing, there was only a boys' bathroom, and I wasn't about to share that cesspool with them.

Now, I had to trudge all the way up to the second floor—to the girls' wing on the west side. I wouldn't even have the opportunity to run into Nym or Razielle, Sarah or Bree, because they were all on the third floor, where I was supposed to be. And since I was now crossing much more than the hallway, I should probably start making sure I had on a bra as well. The last thing I wanted was to give these neophyte horndogs any special *privileges*. The little annoyances.

I took a shower last night to beat the morning rush, so all I had to do was freshen up in the morning. I put on layer upon layer, topping it off with my leather jacket. I even doubled up my socks before pulling on my Docs and lacing them up my ankles. Then I made sure to have Eileen around my neck before heading out the door.

I met up with Nym and Razielle in the lobby. Even though Razielle wasn't in our Morality of Magic class, we still walked with her to the Manor.

Professor Yates smiled when he noticed me

entering the room. "I had a feeling we hadn't seen the last of you," he said, cheerfully.

"You can't get rid of me that easily," I said, taking the seat I'd claimed most of last trimester. "And I think I've received some relevant real-world experience in the Morality of Magic realm."

"I suppose you have," he said. "I suppose you've seen some of the hard choices we as magicals are forced to make."

"Who was it that said absolute power corrupts absolutely?"

Professor Yates brought a hand to his chin as he thought for a moment. "I believe that was John Acton in the 19th century."

"When he was referring to power, he probably wasn't talking about magic, but it seems to totally apply."

"He was referring to the unchecked rule of monarchs—or so it's been interpreted. He could very well have been talking about magic, but it would have been sacrilegious to definitively say so in that day and age. That is why checks and balances are required, as much if not more so in the magical community as in any other established government on Earth. Power, in all its forces, is too sweet a temptress. It's good to have you back, Maeve."

Professor Yates dove into his lesson and it quickly felt like I'd never left. Supernatural History and Lit & Lore went just as smoothly, though I had a good amount of reading to catch up on. I also had some tests to make up, which I was given a week or two to prepare for. I would have to buckle down and get caught up before I could spend too much time detailing the plan with Razielle and Nym to secure the items needed to look for Finley. Rushing to get my needle back wouldn't help me pass my exams, so I needed to prioritize. I needed to be patient, even though patience was not my strong suit, which Finley had told me many times.

Non-Magical Studies with Professor Randell was the one class I didn't feel terribly behind. Even though my brain purged much of the information, most of the class was still review for me.

It was strange having the seat in front of me empty. That was where Finley used to sit. Now I had one more constant reminder that he was gone. We hadn't been here that long, but already, so much of this school reminded me of him, and it tore me apart that he was gone—despite what he did to me.

By the time lunch rolled around, I felt I was getting back into the swing of things. However, I couldn't deny that the morning was heavy on book learning and light on practical magic. The afternoon was where the real challenges lay. I didn't want to let my anxiety ruin my lunch, but I could already feel my stomach tightening into knots.

By the time Nym and I grabbed our food, Razielle, Ivanic, and Bree were already seated at one of the long metal tables. Ivanic was the first to notice me and his whole face lit up like a Christmas tree.

"Well, hello again," I said, setting down my tray and taking a seat beside Razielle.

"Welcome back," Ivanic said. He was seated directly across from me, and Bree next to him. "I knew you'd come back. Didn't I tell you she'd come back?" he asked, gesturing to Bree.

"We were all hopeful," Bree said, greeting me with a smile I wasn't expecting. Perhaps, she wasn't still holding a grudge from last year. "But why did you even leave? I realize it was hard with your brother and all, but you have a whole place here—a home—with or without the extra seamstress powers." She glanced down at my chest, presumably to see if the octagram tattoo was really gone.

"Totally!" Ivanic exclaimed. "You're so one of us now, even if you're still a little peeved about being a neophyte."

"I'm not ashamed of being a freshman again," I said, even though that wasn't the whole truth. "If I was going to college in the fall, I would've had to deal with that there too. But we'll see how well I get through Combative Casting next period. Professor Windsor may literally kill me."

"I told you, you don't have to worry about that. I'll go easy on you," Nym said.

"Yeah, right," I laughed. "You're probably going to

91

get even with me for what I did to you on my first day."

"What did you do to her?" Bree asked, intrigued.

"She just knocked me out of the circle," Nym said. "Which was the assignment."

"I didn't just knock you out of the circle," I said.

"That's it?" Ivanic asked. "I thought it was actually something interesting."

"I threw you like ten feet out of the circle and knocked the wind out of you," I argued.

"I don't think it was that far. And I don't remember it as malicious," Nym said. "But whatever, I won't do the same to you."

"So she says," Razielle said with a mischievous grin. "Those little elves can be tricky bitches."

"Have you met Nym?" I scoffed.

"We've all met Nym," Erik said, taking a seat beside Ivanic. "What are your guys talking about?"

Sarah was with him but decided to take her tray two places down and sit beside Bree. They used to always sit next to each other—practically insepa-rable—finding any opportunity to touch each other. In fact, sometimes it was downright sickening. They suddenly seemed to be two people again, not lost within the guise of a couple. "What did I miss?" I asked, oscillating my gaze between the two of them.

"What do you mean?" Sarah asked, pulling apart half her sandwich to take a bite.

"You two are ten feet apart," I stated like—wasn't this obvious to everyone at the table?

"Yeah…" Erik said, clearly not catching my meaning.

"You two were inseparable before I left and now you're… voluntarily ten feet apart."

"I just had to tell Bree something," Sarah said. "I hadn't realized that was a crime."

"Yeah. We don't have to sit together *all* the time," Erik added.

I scrutinized their seating arrangements again, then said, "You two are finally out of your honeymoon phase, aren't you?"

Erik and Sarah turned to look at each other in horror. "*No…*" they said jointly.

"We're totally still in our honeymoon phase," Erik said.

"We've never been more in love," Sarah said.

"They are saying *I love you* to each other now," Bree interjected.

"We were late to lunch, so we could have a quickie in my room," Erik said.

"*Erik!*" Sarah protested, but she didn't really sound that offended.

"I'm not knocking your relationship. Really. It's maturing. That's all I'm saying," I said, cutting them off before they got too defensive. "I'm happy for you guys. Oh, and did you hear? Nym's gonna kick my ass in Combative Casting. It should be quite the beatdown."

"I *am* not!" Nym argued, sounding more offended than Sarah, and just like that, the conversation moved away from Erik and Sarah's relationship. It was back on me and my inadequacies as a magical.

"It's the quiet ones that punch the hardest," Razielle said.

"I've never punched anyone in my life," Nym said, now looking nervous as all hell.

I put a comforting hand on Nym's back. "Just don't kill me, okay?"

Everyone laughed—except for Nym—and we all kept eating and talking about other things that happened over the winter break. Erik went to Sarah's house and met her family. Ivanic's family vacationed in Aspen. And Bree spent a week on the Mediterranean with her extended family.

I didn't share my whole run-in with the strange girl from Kicryria because I didn't need any more suggestions of what my blood was being used for. The ideas Razielle and Nym had offered were bad enough. I'd already planned to talk with Professor Windsor after class regarding a protection spell, since she was the head neophyte professor.

Despite all the joking, I knew Nym wouldn't rough me up too much. Though I couldn't confidently say the same for Professor Windsor.

CHAPTER 11

"*T*oday, we're going to take what we've been practicing from the previous trimester and really have some fun with it," Professor Windsor exclaimed after we all settled in to class. "I hope you've been practicing over the break.

"We will take our exercise outside, so the elements can play an important role in your focus and concentration. There will be no teams, but every student for themselves. If you are knocked down, then you are out. So, it will be about defense as much as it is offense. You can get hit, but you must remain on your feet. We will continue until there is one student left standing. The grounds between Windsor and Rainley Halls will be the boundaries. Let's go!"

Professor Windsor had welcomed me back when I'd arrived with Nym, but she didn't inquire about

95

my abilities. She'd been in the Crystal Crypt right after I'd lost my needle and my original crystal, so she knew my powers were not what they once were. Perhaps she didn't care. If asked, she'd probably tell me that I was using my needle as a magical crutch, which was what I'd now heard from multiple people.

"I don't like the sound of this," I said to Nym as we exited the classroom. I knew she would go easy on me, but the rest of the class surely wouldn't. In fact, I'd probably be an early target. I supposed it was probably better to get out as soon as possible.

"You'll be fine," she said. "We'll stick together."

"I like the way you think, little elf."

"Maeve," Professor Windsor called from behind me, urging me to stop so she could catch up. "I see you've been given a new crystal. How are you feeling about your abilities since your needle has been taken?"

"Non-existent," I said. "But I just got the new crystal last night, so I haven't gotten much practice with it yet."

"Remember, the needle acted much like the crystal; it amplified powers that were already inherent in you, minus what the needle was capable of on its own, of course. What you practiced in class last trimester was not made possible by the needle but made easier because of the needle. It's an important distinction to remember. With practice, you can cultivate those abilities again. You don't need a needle—you don't need to be a seamstress."

That was easy for her to say. I was the one feeling the enormous gap in my magical abilities since losing the needle. But I understood what she was saying. It was the magical crutch excuse again, and I needed to get past it. In theory, I was now on a more level playing field with the other neophytes, though most of them were still far more seasoned and practiced than I was.

"I'll try to stay positive," I said.

"I know that will be hard but try not to get too discouraged. And I can provide extra help, if you need."

"Actually, I was going to ask you after class about getting a protective spell due to the Kicryrians having a sample of my blood. Maybe something similar to the spell guarding the Crystal Crypt."

Professor Windsor was certainly taken aback by this request, taking her a long moment before responding. "The spell you were continually able to break through?" she finally asked.

I couldn't help but give her a guilty shrug.

"Is the headmistress aware of this?"

"Yes. She came to my apartment to sew up a seam. This black-haired Kicryrian girl broke in, stole my blood, and fled. She wouldn't say what it was for, but I can't imagine it being a good thing."

"What did the headmistress say the blood could be used for?" Professor Windsor asked.

"Not much," I said. "She claimed to not really know why they would want my blood, but I find that hard to believe. I always feel like there are things she's not telling me."

"The headmistress is a skeptical and secretive woman, but it comes with her job—not just as Headmistress of the Academy, but as the head of the Seamstress Counsel. Her mind is filled with a lot of confidential information. I don't envy her for all she's responsible for. It is very likely your blood can be used for some kind of tracking or control spell."

"What about cloning me?" I asked.

"I suppose that is also a possibility, but nothing a protection spell will be able to prevent."

Perfect. I really don't want another version of myself running around.

"The good news is, the Academy's blanket protective spell will already provide a good barrier of defense. I can work on an extra layer of defense for you, but feel I should speak to the headmistress before doing anything."

"If you must," I said with a sigh.

"Headmistress Christi is a good woman. She's on our side—your side."

I guessed there was even privileged information I had that Professor Windsor didn't—like the headmistress willing to steal my needle. However, that was a rather moot point now.

"I'm sure you're right," I said, curious what would come out of her meeting with the headmistress.

When we got outside, the cold hit me like a ton of bricks. I quickly zipped up my leather jacket and pulled a snowcap from the pocket to help keep my ears from totally freezing. It had started to flurry, and the sidewalks and benches were already dusted with snow. Since most classes were in session—*and inside*—the Academy grounds were relatively quiet.

Professor Windsor led us in the sidewalk round-about way to the clearing between Windsor and Rainley Halls.

She gestured with both hands to the snow-covered open space before us. "From the sidewalk to the far one, and to the building on either side—those are your boundaries for this exercise.

"It's freezing out here," one student complained.

"That makes it harder, doesn't it?" the professor said with a chuckle. "You'll have to divide your focus between staying warm, defending yourself, and attacking your opponent. Now spread out. When I shoot a light into the air, then it will be your signal to start."

The lot of us left the relatively cleared sidewalk and ventured into the powdery snow, fanning out across the large field. Nym stuck right by my side and we tried to steer clear from everyone else.

"If it somehow gets down to just the two of us, then go ahead and take me out," I said.

"If it gets down to just the two of us, then I consider us both winners," Nym said between chattering teeth.

"But there can be only one, little elf." My teeth were chattering just as much as hers, and it felt like every muscle in my body was contracting from the cold. It was a workout just to stand still.

Then a flash caught my attention and I saw a bright blue spark shoot from Professor Windsor's extended forefinger. The energy bolt shot straight up into the air like a missile, then burst into a glittery explosion fifty feet overhead. That was the signal. And I could see the hesitation from the rest of the class as nobody immediately moved.

But all it took was one energy ball to fire, one student to hit the snow, before everyone else jumped into action and fought like their lives depended on it.

CHAPTER 12

*P*rofessor Windsor had strongly implied that the object of the exercise was to take down other classmates by magical means, but it was not explicitly expressed. With my abilities so severely hindered, physically taking others down seemed like my only viable alternative—not to mention it was something I knew I could do.

There's always more than one way to play a game. But we'd see how long Professor Windsor would allow me to get away with this strategy.

As soon as different colored and sized energy balls burst into existence and flew through the air, many students were running for some type of cover, of which there was a very limited supply. Only several topiaries and benches resided in this area to shield attacks.

Nym and I stayed by the edge and no one immediately charged us. Despite what I knew about my
abilities, there still seemed to be an intimidation
factor surrounding me—one I needed to use to my
advantage until it became general knowledge I was
shooting blanks.

"Nym, I need you to fire at anyone who
approaches us," I said. "While you have them focused
on blocking your attacks, I'll come in from the side
and throw them to the ground."

"How?" she asked, her voice trembling from
concern as much as the cold.

"The way I've always done it up to this point," I
said. "By getting physical."

"But Professor Windsor said—"

"Nope," I said, cutting her off. "She didn't. Now
stay alert. We're not going down so easily. Are you
with me?"

Nym nodded nervously.

Then two orange fireballs flew between us—one
right after the other—almost knocking each of us off
balance. I spun to see a blond boy aiming his palms
in our direction—one at each of us. He released
another two fireballs before Nym returned a shot. I
ducked, the energy ball whizzing right by my ear.
Nym successfully blocked the one aimed at her.

With the boy now preoccupied with Nym, I ran
out of the line of fire, appearing to be running away
—until I made a sharp turn and charged the boy

from the side. He didn't notice me coming for him until I was a few steps away, and by that time, he couldn't get off another shot.

I slid my foot behind his legs and shoved him hard. He had no chance for recovery once he started to tumble backward, landing hard on his ass in the ankle-deep snow.

"Hey!" he yelled. "That has to be a foul!"

"I'll allow it," the voice of Professor Windsor boomed. She was now standing on the head of a grizzly bear topiary up on its hind legs, overlooking the whole scene. "I'm sorry, Scotty, but you're out."

"Man!" Scotty protested, hammering a fist into the snow before getting up and moping toward the sidewalk where other losers were already gathering.

I glanced up at Professor Windsor, who was still focused on Nym and me, seemingly curious of our strategy and how it would ultimately play out.

"Maeve, watch out!" Nym cried.

Not knowing where the threat was coming from, I instinctively ducked, but an energy ball still hit me square in the back. The impact threw me forward, but I landed on my hands. To roll with the momentum, I wanted to somersault, then spring to my feet, but I knew that would take me out of the competition. So, I absorbed the impact, scrambled to my feet, and darted to the side, anticipating another shot not far behind.

Once I was able to assess where Nym was and

who was attacking us, I saw two girls also working as a team to take us out. One fired at Nym while the other focused on me. I just had to remain standing long enough for Nym to win her battle and aid me with taking down the girl named Yolanda, who was readying herself to fire at me again.

"Nice shot, Nym!" I exclaimed. And just as I'd expected, Yolanda glanced back to check on her teammate who was still battling it out with Nym. I took advantage of Yolanda's momentary distraction and charged her like I had with Scotty.

However, Yolanda saw me coming much earlier than Scotty had. I was also coming at her head-on instead of from the side, but I had no choice but to stay the course. Still a fair distance away, I was easily able to dodge her next shot. It took her time to gather the energy and focus for creating another fireball, and it was obvious that I was wrecking her concentration. Before she was able to shoot at me again, I rammed her at full speed, sending her helpless body collapsing into the snow. Yolanda nearly pulled me down with her, but I broke away before she was able to solidify her hold.

Seconds after I took out Yolanda, Nym knocked her teammate to the ground with a double energy ball.

"Now, *that* was a nice shot!" I said, laughing as the other two girls proceeded on the walk of shame to the sidewalk. Nym gave me a guilty smile, still unsure of what to make of this whole exercise.

No more shots were careening toward my head, so I glanced around the area to identify our next threat or target. And as I surveyed who remained, I quickly realized we were already in the top half of the class. Professor Windsor was still observing from her perch atop the snow-covered bear, strangely reminding me of the time I'd noticed Otis sitting on the roof of the Hollywood High gymnasium—at the time when everything in my life started getting weird. And it hadn't stopped yet.

As I looked over the makeshift battlefield with more confidence than when the exercise began, I finally noticed a tingling at my chest. I became acutely aware that my teeth weren't chattering any longer. The crystal against my skin felt warm for the first time since Devon had given it to me yesterday. Maybe I was finally connecting to its power, to the extra power Eileen was supplying me with.

The tingling sensation flowed from my chest and down my arms, filling me with a warmth I hadn't felt since losing the crystal housing my mother's soul. I didn't know who this Eileen was, but I felt a calmness emanating from the crystal.

"Are you okay?" Nym asked.

I must have looked like I was spacing out, which wasn't comforting for my teammate at a time like this. I brought my attention back to Nym and our combative surroundings.

"I'm here," I said. "I can feel the power of the crystal. It's not nearly as strong as before, but it's there."

"That's great news!" she said. "Do you think you can conjure an energy ball?"

"Let's not get ahead of ourselves. I can feel a bit of energy and don't feel like I'm going to die from the cold anymore, but I don't know about conjuring anything yet."

"Stop selling yourself short. Now's the time to try. See what you can do. Put some of that fight back into the magic."

I knew she was right. If I had as much faith in my magical abilities as I did in my physical abilities, then I'd be back to throwing fireballs with the best in the class in no time, but there was still an unnatural feeling to it. I still felt like I didn't totally belong without my needle.

But as we remained standing in our corner of the battlefield debating my abilities, the remaining students were on the offensive. Three more students had teamed up and were heading our way. The bitter students I'd taken out were griping from the sidelines, which had caught the attention of students still in the game. My physical takedowns were not being well received. Nym and I were swiftly becoming the common enemy. And it was clear they were mostly coming for me. Of the three students descending upon us, one went to occupy Nym's attention while two confronted me.

Bring it on, bitches.

The guy and girl attacking me spread out. If I went for one, the other could continue the assault from an advantageous vantage point. The guy shot a green energy ball toward my head. As soon as I ducked, the girl shot a ball of white light aimed at my midsection. I dodged it, but there was already another one coming by the time I found my footing.

"Nym, a little help here!" I shouted.

"Shoot back!" Nym said.

The warmth in my hands felt familiar, but every time I tried to concentrate on calling forth an energy ball to fling back at my attackers, I was interrupted by another ball seeking to drop me into the snow.

They both saw my weakness and it became apparent why I'd been doing physical attacks up until now. My magic wasn't working. Whatever impressive things I did in class earlier in the year seemed to be no longer applying.

"Keep shooting!" the guy yelled. "She can't keep dancing forever!"

"The hell I can't!" I shot back, dodging another one of their energy missiles. "I can do this all day!" Except I couldn't. I was already getting tired. And my fatigue was also hindering my attempts at rediscovering my magic.

My movements were already becoming slower and less graceful. Then one of the fiery white balls slammed into my shoulder, spinning me around, but not knocking me off my feet. Pain radiated down my arm, causing one whole side of my body to ache.

Then another impact hit me square in the ass—this one originating from the guy. I didn't know if it was intentional or simply a lucky shot, but it made my blood boil.

"Hey, watch where you're aiming those things!" I roared. And as I extended my aching arm to point a menacing finger in his direction, an orange bullet-sized projectile shot from my finger and hit him in the center of his chest, knocking him backward a few steps. As he stumbled, he seemed to trip over his own feet, sending him sprawling into the snow.

I couldn't believe what I'd done! The force of my shot was nowhere near as intense as before, but I'd still shot an energy ball from my finger without my needle. And it wasn't a strictly mental change like the possibility of adapting to the cold. There really was still magic inside of me like my friends had said. I could do this!

I turned to where Nym had been fighting, hoping she'd seen what I'd just done, but I found her in the snow as well—and her attacker aiming at me.

I braced myself for the shot just as I was hit in the back by the girl I'd also been squaring off with. I stumbled forward, then was hit by another energy ball from the side. I teetered to the side just as I was hit in the back again, then from a direction I hadn't been anticipating at all. The shots seemed to suddenly be coming from everywhere. My feet were no longer under me and I joined my teammate in the snow, my knees buckling, then my body crumpling to the ground like a puppet whose strings had been cut.

When I was finally able to make sense of what had happened to me, I saw five satisfied faces staring down at me.

Where the hell had they all come from?

"I'm sorry, Maeve," Nym said as she climbed to her feet. "I tried to get back to help you."

I sat up in the snow, a little dazed, as the five remaining students dispersed and continued to fight for supremacy.

It sucked to be out, but we'd made it much farther than I'd originally anticipated—and I regained a bit of my magic, which was a huge win. The pain was secondary next the new feeling of euphoria. I could start to believe it again. I could start to see what was possible for me, even without the needle—showing me what was possible all along.

I shook my head and slowly got to my feet. As I did so, I looked up at the topiary bear, where Professor Windsor was still standing. With a nod and a slight smile, she confirmed what I was feeling

—that I had accomplished a great feat and should be proud.

"There's no reason to be sorry," I said to Nym, as I joined her to return to the sidewalk. "We did awesome. *You* did awesome."

However, as soon as I'd said it, I heard laughter coming from another section of the sidewalk, not where the rest of our class was gathered. In a small cluster stood a group of Master Classmen over-looking the game, but now mostly focused on Nym and me. All of them wore soul crystals that shone brightly in the afternoon sun.

"Yeah; that was *awesome*," one of the guys said. "Awesomely bad."

"I think that was the smallest energy ball I've ever seen," another said.

"You're like the oldest neophyte this Academy's ever had," one of the girls added.

I knew engaging them would only get me into trouble, especially with this being my first day back and Professor Windsor right there. Devon's urge for me to stay out of trouble also rang loudly in my ears, though it was tough to ignore their jeers and taunts.

"Don't listen to them," Nym said, grabbing my arm to keep me moving toward the rest of the class.

However, I recognized two of the Master Classmen as being in the group that jumped Finley. More may have been there. I couldn't remember their faces clearly enough now. It had been dark, and

Guy had downed the entire group with a single wave of energy.

"Fuck off," I spat back at the group, then allowed Nym to lead me to higher ground while the laughter continued to sound behind us.

CHAPTER 13

*T*he group of Master Classmen were still hanging out when Professor Windsor walked us back inside, but they were gone by the time class was over and Nym and I returned to Windsor Hall.

"You're still thinking about them, aren't you?" Nym asked as we strolled down the snow-dusted sidewalk with a flood of other students who'd all been released from class.

"Thinking about who?" I asked, knowing full well who she was talking about. I wanted to sound like I was above it, even though the tone of my voice probably told otherwise.

"I can see the gears in your mind spinning and grinding. If you let them get to you, then they'll just keep coming."

"I know how to handle bullies," I said. "I've been

doing it all my life."

"Yeah, you fight them—except your magical abilities aren't on par with your physical abilities."

"Thanks for reminding me. I'm fully aware of my magical inadequacies."

"I'm not trying to be mean but trying to help."

"How is telling me I suck magically helpful?"

"I didn't tell you… never mind. I'm sorry I said anything." Nym's sad gaze veered away from me.

I caught her arm and forced her to stop. "God, Nym. Don't just crumble. Speak your mind. I don't mean to jump down your throat, but I'm going to respond. That's not your cue to back down from what you were trying to say."

"I'm sorry. I didn't mean—"

"And stop apologizing for having an opinion. Freakin' own it, girl," I insisted.

"I—I'm trying to," she said, her voice a little shaky, which I assumed was from the cold. "You can just be intense sometimes."

"I know. And that intensity is going to bring my magic back—back to full strength. Just watch. Today is just the beginning."

"I believe you," she said, her lips curling up into a fearful smile. "I believe you can do anything. Not like me."

"And stop selling yourself short," I admonished. "You told me that, remember? What you did today was nothing short of amazing. You just have to believe it too. I can't do all the believing for you."

"You're right."

"No shit, I'm right," I laughed, feeling pumped and more confident than ever if I had to deal with those Master Classmen again.

I went with Nym back to our—her—room and met up with Razielle. The bunk bed I'd shared with Nym was gone, replaced by a second twin bed. And it turned out that this was how the room was arranged at the beginning of the school year, before there was any thought of me entering the picture.

"The room looks so empty without the bunk," I said, looking around, feeling almost like I'd been erased.

"Certainly missing something," Razielle said. "But whatcha gonna do?"

I shrugged because there really *wasn't* anything else to do.

"The desks look different too," I said.

"They were replaced after the room had been trashed."

I'd remembered the girls mentioning the room being turned upside down—someone searching for any clue of where I'd gone—which resulted in that Quin girl receiving one of Ben's envelopes with a return address. I still couldn't believe I'd been so careless. At least my roommates hadn't turned me in.

"That wasn't cool," I said. "Sorry, you two had to go through that."

"We survived," Razielle said in her typical sarcastic fashion.

"Clothes and stuff can be easily replaced," Nym added. It was easy for her to say since her family was rich—well, both girls' families were.

We headed down to the basement a few minutes early. Bree was the only one there besides Devon, and I knew better than to simply cut into their conversation. Bree and I seemed to finally be back on good terms, and I wanted to keep it that way.

As the three of us entered the room, Devon turned his attention my way and smiled. We took our seats as Bree continued to talk his ear off, and every so often, he glanced over at me. I didn't know if he was trying to get me to save him or just wanted to look at me, but I had no intention of interrupting.

The others filed in shortly after—Ivanic, followed by Erik and Sarah.

Ivanic took a seat next to me. "Just like old times," he said with a sly smirk.

"Have you found yourself a girlfriend yet?" I asked.

"Just waiting for the right one to return."

"Maybe you should be looking at someone who never left." Then I leaned in closer. "What about Razielle? She seems into you, and she's not bad to look at, right?"

"On paper, she's perfect," Ivanic said. "But I just don't feel it."

"You could still give her a chance. Maybe she'll grow on you."

He didn't skip a beat. "I believe the same will apply to you and me. You'll see."

I couldn't help but to laugh at his unwavering bravado. "I'm with Devon."

"Are you, really?"

As far as I knew, but I didn't want to come off unsure with Ivanic ready to pounce like the puma he was. "Yes," I simply said.

"I like the guy and all, but you can do better. You'll come to realize that one day." Ivanic smiled wide and leaned back in his chair.

"You're something else," I said, still laughing.

"I know, right?"

"Are we ready to get started?" Devon asked, addressing the small class, still seated atop the professor's desk.

"Yes, please," I blurted out, needing to stop Ivanic from talking before he ended up proposing to me.

We paired up and I was back to working with Devon, so I exchanged my desk for one closer to the professor's.

"How's it going?" Devon asked once I was situated.

"Did you get everything you needed done last

night?" I asked. I wasn't still bitter about him leaving after I'd asked him to stay… potentially for the night. Okay; I was totally bitter, and I wanted him to sense it.

Devon shifted uncomfortably in the desk he'd pulled next to mine. "For the most part," he said. "I wish I could have stayed longer, and I hope to make it up to you."

"I have a lot of catching up to do, so whatever you have planned will probably have to wait until this weekend." I needed to make sure I took back some control of the situation. I needed him to understand he had to work around my schedule too. I couldn't let him think I'd be patiently waiting around and jump on the first chance *he* was free. He needed to wait for *me* to be free.

"I understand," he said, looking a little disappointed—which was a good thing in my eyes. "We'll work something out. If you want to keep the extra study sessions going after this, then I'm happy to do so."

"They're not mandatory anymore?"

Devon shook his head. "The headmistress isn't requiring that anymore. It was originally mandated to help you extract your needle. That's not exactly an objective anymore."

"I'm not special enough anymore," I said.

"You're not a seamstress anymore. To me, that doesn't make you any less special. But the headmistress will no longer be keeping such a close eye on your progress."

"Well, that's one good thing to come out of all this. And public displays of affection won't be so taboo anymore?"

"I'd still rather not in front of my students," Devon said. "It feels weird."

"*I'm* one of your students," I countered.

"You know what I mean." He sighed and reached for a tablet on the professor's desk. "Let's see what you need to catch up on, shall we?"

"*Everything*," I said and retrieved my own tablet from my bag.

"I don't think we need to worry much about Non-Magical Studies. That's stuff you can review on your own or with your roommates."

"I don't have roommates anymore, remember? I'm *all alone*." I intended for it to sound dramatic, even though I thought I was going to enjoy my own space. "Oh, and before I forget, can you give me the last name of the woman in my crystal?"

"Why?"

"I want to know."

"I don't know it."

"Can you get it?"

He ran a frustrated hand through his hair and I could tell I was wearing him down. "You shouldn't look too much into it. Just accept her as your aide."

"I didn't ask questions last time and look what

happened," I said, challenging him to even attempt to argue that fact.

"I'll get you a name," Devon finally said, then swiped his finger across the tablet. "Are you ready to focus now?"

"I'm always focused—you may just disagree with what I'm focused on." I smirked at him, causing him to shake his head.

Throughout the rest of the hour, we went through assignments and pre-tests for Supernatural History and Lit & Lore. There was a lot of reading I had to do on my own, but it didn't seem like I had missed as much as I'd feared.

I told the others I'd catch up with them at dinner when their time was up. As much as I'd given Devon a hard time earlier in the class, I was still looking forward to my alone time with him. Ivanic was the last one to leave and I almost had to push him out the door.

"You kids behave," he admonished as I closed and bolted the door behind him. He gave me an *I'm watching you* glare through the glass before leaving to catch up with the others.

When I turned, Devon was only a few steps away. I marched right up to him and planted my lips on his. He pulled me in and wrapped his strong arms around me, squeezing me tight like I might disappear again. I melted into his hold as I savored the sweetness of his lips. But I had to keep myself from being completely pulled underwater. I couldn't fully melt and lose myself in him. I needed to remain strong—and leave him wanting more.

I pulled back my lips while he did everything he could to reconnect himself to my breath of life. I placed my hands firmly on his chest and forced space between us.

"What's the matter?" he asked once he realized I wouldn't relent.

"Nothing," I said. "But I'm staying after so you can help me."

"I thought you were staying after so we could spend more time together," Devon said with a pout, which was rather comical.

"Can't it be both?" I broke free of his grasp and stepped back, beyond his reach.

"You have no idea what you do to me."

You didn't seem to feel that last night. "If you want me to be able to stay, then I need to improve," I said instead. "I need to get back up to par in Combative Casting. I'm already losing my edge. After today, the other students know I'm practically shooting blanks."

"The fact that you could shoot anything at all is a powerful first step," Devon said, his demeanor changing as he seemed to get back on board with our lesson. "When you were finally able to conjure an energy ball, what were you feeling?"

"Furious because this one guy had just shot me in the ass."

"I'll kill him!" Devon barked, then laughed.

"It wasn't funny," I argued.

"I realize it wasn't in the moment, which was how you were able to harness the power. Your anger is powerful, it always has been. It seems to be the easiest way for you to fully focus. You don't get distracted and overwhelmed when you're furious but dial in to a laser-like focus. And that's how you're able to feel the power that, at other times, is just a few inches out of your reach. Remember when you threw the desk at me?"

"How could I forget?" I said, a smile creeping onto my face. "You made me just as furious as anyone."

"Go back to that place," Devon insisted. "Dig deep and find the rage. Later, you can experiment with different emotions—but for now, your rage seems to be the most effective."

"I can't just flip a switch and go back there."

"You'll have to." Devon took a few steps back from me, gestured with one hand, and one of the desks came skidding across the carpet, aimed directly at me.

I barely had a chance to jump to the side before the schoolroom projectile crashed into two more desks beside me.

"Hey, watch it, mister!" I warned. "You nearly hit me."

"I guess I need to try harder," Devon said, his expression morphing from lighthearted playfulness to pure determination.

Before I had a chance to react, two more desks were launched in my direction. I dodged one just before the other crashed into me, knocking me to the floor. I was barely able to keep my head from bouncing off the not-so-padded carpet.

"What the hell, man!" I yelled as I sprang to my feet. I wasn't going to wait for another desk to come barreling in my direction while I was lying helplessly on the floor.

"Attack me with an energy ball," Devon ordered.

"Are you trying to make me mad?"

"Is it working?"

"Yeah!"

"Then do something about it, Rhodes."

I glanced around to see which desk was coming for me next. Nothing moved—but then I was hit from behind as one of the desks from before came skidding in the opposite direction. This one didn't hit me as hard, so I was able to remain on my feet, but I was furious nonetheless.

I felt the warmth at my chest, which quickly spread across my shoulders and down my arms. I focused intently on my palms, willing an energy ball to burst to life. I could feel it and see it, but it still seemed to be just beyond the physical world.

"Come on, Rhodes! Attack me!"

I was angry with him, but still knew it was an act to antagonize me. A part of me still didn't want to attack him, even though these were the exercises we did in Combative Casting. I'd had to work through the same struggles with Nym, afraid I was going to hurt her. I didn't want to delude myself into thinking Devon couldn't handle whatever I threw his way... but something was still holding me back.

Now there were three chairs creeping toward me from different directions. They were like wild animals getting in position before jumping in for the kill. He was going to launch one or more of them at any second.

I remained focused on my hands, which now felt like they were on fire, yet still no balls of fire burst from my skin.

One desk rocketed toward me and I knocked it aside with my useless hands. I raised my palms again just as the other two leaped forward like wolves on their prey. One missed me, but the final one crashed directly into me, falling onto me as I tumbled backward. Just when I thought I was going to be pinned under the metal beast, it soared to one side and crashed into the wall.

Devon was at my side in a flash. "Are you okay?" he asked, his determination replaced by concern.

I felt tears prickling the edges of my eyes, but I was determined as hell not to cry in front of him.

Don't you dare, Rhodes.

But I was so frustrated and overwhelmed knowing where I'd been and seeing where I was now. It was night and day. I wanted to scream to deter the tears from taking over. I wasn't a crier, but everyone had their breaking point. It didn't seem like a significant moment, but it was the culmination of everything that had happened over the past month that was dragging me to the cliff, where I was now teetering at the edge.

"You need to let me know when it's too much," Devon said when I didn't answer him.

I simply shook my head and wiped my eyes before he noticed any tears. "I'm fine," I said. "Just angry with myself, not you."

"You were supposed to get angry with *me*."

"I tried… I just couldn't get there."

"It's okay," Devon said. "We can take a step back. There are other things we can work on." He leaned forward and kissed the top of my head, which for some reason made me angrier than everything else he'd thrown at me.

CHAPTER 14

*D*evon said he'd meet the rest of us in the cafeteria. He came back with me to my room, where I could drop off my bag before heading off to dinner. I zipped up my leather jacket, anticipating the biting cold, which was so much worse once we stepped outside.

"Maybe you should invest in a proper winter coat," Devon said when he saw me shivering.

"I'll survive," I said, determined to get to the point where I could regulate my temperature again. Until then, I'd suffer.

The cloud cover overhead was thick, and it was beginning to snow. The two of us walked briskly down the meandering sidewalks, but we parted ways as we drew close to the Manor, so he could stop off at his room first.

"I'll save you a seat," I said as we parted with a

lingering grasp between our two hands. At several paces, our fingers slipped from one another, and we continued down our separate paths.

As I approached the cafeteria, I became acutely aware of footsteps behind me, without the prattling of casual conversation—someone who seemed to be keeping pace with me. There were plenty of students here and plenty that walked alone, even after dark, but something about the gait from behind me made the hair on the back of my neck rise to attention.

I slowed my pace to see if the person behind me would simply pass and continue in the direction of the cafeteria.

The footsteps drew closer, quickly coming up beside me, which allowed me to exhale the breath I'd unknowingly been holding.

As I glanced over, an unexpected hand reached toward me—expertly finding the chain of my crystal. In one smooth motion, the necklace split and was yanked off my neck. The skin of my neck burned like I'd been whipped, the bitter cold making it that much worse.

"You don't deserve this," the boy said and kept right on walking, the crystal dangling at his side, now glowing a brilliant blue.

I hadn't gotten a good look at him, but swore he was in the group that had been taunting me toward the end of Combative Casting.

"Are you fucking kidding me?" I called after him.

Instead of engaging, the boy sped up and veered off the sidewalk, into the ankle-high snow away from the cafeteria.

I didn't think twice about running after him, and when he heard me crunching through the snow behind him, he broke into a run as well, into the darkness of the open grounds. There was no way he was getting away with *my* crystal. The gall of him snatching it right off my neck made me livid.

It was clear I was faster than he was, and I quickly closed the gap between us. I reached out to grab for the back of his coat as we passed one of the many topiaries—and in the next moment, I was toppling forward, face-first into the snow. My foot had snagged something I hadn't noticed in the darkness.

And when the boy heard me fall, he didn't continue to race away as I'd expected, but slowed and turned. The necklace was still dangling from his hand, the glistening crystal swinging like a tiny pendulum.

Suddenly, my whole body tensed, instantly realizing what was happening. I glanced back and saw a figure step away from the topiary of a wizard.

"There are no special privileges... especially for a neophyte," said the boy who'd tripped me.

Then I saw five or six more Master Classmen gathering around me, including the boy I'd been chasing. It was hard to make them all out in the darkness, especially with most of them wearing fur-trimmed hoods. But the boy who'd tripped me didn't even need a coat. He was simply wearing a black long-sleeved shirt. He was trim and tall, and his dark, straight hair blew wildly in the wind.

I could only imagine how Finley had been feeling when a group like this descended upon him for having a crystal—*my* crystal. Even with the crystal, his powers were weak, like mine now. I knew they were here to haze me, and I needed to act fast if I wanted to get out of this without too much humiliation.

"If you're going to attend the premier magical academy in the country, you should at least have some magical ability," the boy without the coat said. He had been there this afternoon and I was pretty sure he was one of the fallen students I'd kicked after Finley's attack. With this being the first time he'd come after me, I was guessing he didn't remember that small detail.

"I saw her fight in the village, so keep your distance," a girl said from behind me. "She's devilishly fast."

"We'll see how fast she is when she's freezing her ass off," no-coat guy said.

Oh, hell no!

I didn't waste a moment before lunging for him. No-coat guy was obviously in charge, and I knew that groups of bullies would usually scatter by simply conquering the leader. And focusing on one person was the best way to ensure I inflicted some real damage, which I fully intended to do. He was mine and I'd use whatever means necessary to take him down. I'd have to ask for forgiveness from the Academy powers-that-be later.

Unfortunately for him, no-coat guy thought he had more time to insult me before I'd strike. He released dual energy balls, which he'd expected would throw me backward. They probably should have, but my momentum wouldn't allow anything to stop me now. They hit me square in the chest, but I kept coming—I wouldn't be deterred by pain. I tackled him before he could shoot me again, and as the two of us went down, I connected a knee with his crotch—*hard*.

He grunted in pain, with an awkward squeal also escaping his lips. Then as our bodies collided upon hitting the ground, my forehead smashed into his cheek. A crack rang out in the frozen evening air, then a tortured cry.

As dazed as I was from the impact, I still felt the cold bite on my limbs—bare skin touching the snow. It was suddenly much colder than it had been a moment before. I pushed up off the guy, trying to escape the increased cold only to discover I had practically nothing protecting my skin from the harsh elements.

My leather jacket was gone. My Docs were gone.

My clothes had disappeared. No one had ripped them off, but I was suddenly lying on the snow-covered ground in my underwear—just like Finley had been.

I sprang up in a panic, and my bare feet sinking into the ankle-high snow was torturous. They wanted to give out, but I knew what awaited me if they did. I couldn't handle any more exposed skin being kissed by the merciless snow.

The boy before me continued to groan, not comprehending what had happened to me, but laughter rang out from the others behind. They weren't scattering.

"It's a little chilly out here," someone said.

"Sure is; and it's only going to get colder as it gets later," someone else said.

I spun around, wrapping my arms around my body, like it would provide any warmth. I scanned the group of onlookers for whoever was holding my clothes. Someone must have them. They couldn't just be gone. However, the only thing I saw anyone holding was my crystal, and it was well out of reach and might as well be a thousand miles away.

"How're you feeling now, neophyte?" one of the girls asked. "Having a hard time breathing?"

I *was* having a hard time breathing. My teeth were chattering so hard, I couldn't even verbalize a response. Every muscle in my body was flexed to the max and was now out of my control. I wanted to attack every one of these girls, but the thought of anything else touching my body was agonizing. I no longer had my needle, but felt the pinpricks everywhere. I had no idea how long I'd be able to last in this cold before my body completely shut down.

They were surrounding me, so I couldn't even make a run for it without confronting someone.

"Go ahead," a different girl said. "It's so obvious what you're thinking."

F—f—f—uck, it's freakin' freezing.

In the moment, I didn't even care what I was showing off to these assholes. My underwear wasn't even matching, not that I had many matching sets.

I tried to assess who was the weakest link in the circle, but in their dark, hooded coats they all looked so similar. I could only distinguish one of the girls from her voice. In the end, I just had to choose.

However, before I could get two raw steps, I was hit with another energy ball, which hurt so much more without my leather jacket to insulate the blow. It stopped me in my tracks—then when another ball hit me in the side, I couldn't stop from dropping to my knees.

"Oh, come on, stay awhile. We're just having a little fun." This was a male voice, but I couldn't even tell from which direction it was coming as the extreme pain was setting in and completely clouding my mind.

My knees were on fire, but my thighs shook, and

I couldn't seem to return to my feet no matter how much I wanted to.

It also dawned on me that along with my clothes, my phone was gone. I figured someone had to have it since Finley hadn't lost his phone in his attack, though I assumed Guy had somehow gotten it back.

Where was Devon? Why was he not coming back, passing by on his way to the cafeteria and coming to save me? Finley had Guy and me. And I seemed to have no one. I wouldn't think they'd leave me out here to die, but who knew what these assholes were capable of? Maybe they were Kicryrians too.

I somehow found the strength to get back to my feet, though my legs could barely hold my own weight. And my symbol of strength only brought on an onslaught of more fiery balls from all directions, dropping me back to the snow.

My fingers and toes were going numb, and there was nothing I could do about it. I couldn't warm myself and couldn't escape. I couldn't fight my way out of this kind of pain. Unable to even remain on my knees, I toppled over, reduced to the fetal position in the snow.

"Do you get your place yet?" one of the girls asked. "You're at the bottom of the food chain. It doesn't matter how high you think you are among the Norms—among the magicals, you're nothing."

"Get her up," the voice of no-coat guy

commanded. He appeared in my periphery, back on his feet. Dried blood was smeared across his face, but it seemed that the damage I'd inflicted had worn off.

Two sets of gloved hands grabbed my arms and hauled me to my feet. Now that my body was damp from the snow, the icy wind burned that much more. I could barely feel my legs anymore and couldn't stand on my own. I wanted to fight them, but my body wouldn't cooperate. Now that I knew what he'd gone through, Finley seemed to have endured the torture better than I was doing. And I was the strong one!

"Bring her over here," no-coat said, and I was dragged quickly toward the wizard topiary.

My feet tried to keep up with the two guys carrying me, but they were practically useless by this point.

The two guys fought to prop me up against the side of the topiary, but my legs were jelly beneath me. However, I felt more arms snaking around my body, helping to hold me up. Then the two guys that had been carrying me stepped away, leaving me supported by the mysterious new arms.

As I painfully turned my head, I discovered what was now holding me up. Branches from the topiary had come alive like tentacles and snaked themselves around my arms. More reached out for my torso, then slithered around my frozen legs.

I was about to scream in terror as one more branch inched around my neck and pulled tight—not enough to cut off my air supply completely, but firm enough to act as a warning not to scream. Then I was lifted completely off the ground, suspended in midair from the monstrous arms.

"This is what happens to neophytes that don't belong," no-coat guy said, his face now inches from mine, his angry eyes boring into my glassy ones. "By the time anyone finds you, you'll just be another permanent frozen fixture on the Academy grounds." Then he walked away, followed by the other hooded figures in his group.

I struggled against the tight branches, but instantly learned how futile it was. Every movement was agony and was in no way getting me closer to escaping.

Someone will walk by. I know it's dark, but someone will walk by and see me...

I had to convince myself that someone would find me, and I wasn't going to freeze to death out here.

However, as I repeated the mantra that I'd be saved, the branches tightened even more—no, not tightened, but pulled. To my horror, they began to pull me into the topiary. And within moments, the snowy wizard had swallowed me whole.

CHAPTER 15

*A*s I disappeared from view, I tried my damnedest to scream, but could only get out raspy gurgles due to the branch squeezing my windpipe. I fought harder than I ever had before, desperate to break the shrubbery monster's powerful grip. My numbing skin tore as I rubbed it feverously against the bark. If I could just free one limb, then I'd know my situation wasn't completely hopeless.

I continued to fight for my life, doing whatever I could to wake the limbs that were succumbing to the long winter night. But it seemed to be a losing battle.

As I fought the branches, more snow shook free from overhead and rained down on top of me. And the limbs refused to loosen their relentless hold.

I couldn't believe this was how I was going to die

—at the hands of some senior bullies. I'd been in some one-sided fights in my life, but I was always able to swing the odds in my direction. I fought dirty and was never completely out.

But how did you fight dirty against an enchanted bush? I couldn't get inside its head. I couldn't knee it in the balls. I couldn't even successfully bite it, for God's sake.

Fear was settling deep in my gut. I was never going to find out what happened to Finley. I was never going to learn the truth about my parents. I was never going to realize my true powers. And I wouldn't even have the opportunity to say goodbye to my friends.

But as the fear continued to make itself at home, my anger finally began to return. I couldn't go out like this. I always told Finley never to quit and here I was doing just that. It was rage that gave me power. That was how I'd survived several daunting falls. That was how I'd conjured an energy ball earlier today.

Maybe I could signal to someone that way. If only I could release an energy ball into the air like a beacon for help, someone would see it and come running.

Where there's a will, there's a way. You're not helpless, Rhodes. If you truly believe you're helpless, then this place will be your goddamn tomb!

With the last of my strength, I somehow

managed to ignite a fire within myself. Even without the crystal, my chest grew warm, then radiated throughout my body. It felt like a shell of ice covering my body was melting away. As my palms heated more, I pictured one of those energy balls in my mind. I just needed to be able to launch it through the dense foliage overhead, so it could get someone's attention.

I concentrated as hard as I could—blocking out all the pain, numbness, inhibitions, and threat of freezing to death—until a tiny sun in the palm of my hand was all I could see.

And miraculously, my hands began to glow.

I'm doing it!

They burned with the energy of an inner flame until a brilliant ball materialized inches from my open hand.

However, instead of launching upward, the ball singed the closest branch, and as it recoiled, the bark was set ablaze.

One arm was instantly freed as the branch tried to escape the growing flames. I withdrew my arm as well to keep from being burned.

Then a fireball burst to life from my other palm and ignited the branch holding that arm. As the fire quickly spread, all the branches wound tightly around my body retreated farther into the topiary.

I dropped to the ground on numb legs that were unable to support me. I fell forward, through the regular branches that clawed and scratched me as my body toppled out of the confines of the wizard just as he truly started to go up in flames.

The biting cold was almost as bad as the growing flames, but I knew the fire would do more damage sooner than the cold, so I scrambled through the snow to reach a safe distance.

I glanced back at the wizard topiary now engulfed in bright orange flames. There was my beacon, calling to everyone in the surrounding buildings. And I so wanted to get the hell out of here —*stat*.

A small portion of the fire was still inside of me, slowly thawing my numb, scratched, and sore limbs. I pushed up on my hands and knees, then up onto my feet. A trail of blood marked where I'd crawled away from the wizard, my body covered in scrapes and cuts. My legs shook as I took the first few steps, then crashed back into the snow.

I fought my way back to my feet again and stumbled forward a few more steps before falling again. By the third time, I was able to remain on my feet and hobbled all the way to the sidewalk, out of the ankle-deep snow.

Students were starting to spill from the surrounding buildings, curious of the now raging fire on school grounds. I glanced down at my nearly naked body, marred like I'd scaled barbed wire, and made a run for Windsor Hall, which was still several buildings away. As I ran, I was finally able to pick up speed until I reached a full sprint on bare feet, ignoring the stabs of pain shooting up through my soles. I didn't stop as I crashed through the front door and raced past some unsuspecting neophytes as I made a beeline for my dorm room.

It didn't occur to me that I had no key to even get into my room until I reached the door. I slammed into it with both fists, which hurt like hell as they prickled with countless needles as my skin adjusted to the interior warmth.

Shit!

All I could think of doing was running upstairs and hiding in the third-floor girls' bathroom until Nym and Razielle returned from dinner. Then at least I could borrow some clothes, so I could see Professor Windsor about getting a new key for my room. Then I'd have to figure out what to do about my phone… and my crystal… and those jackasses that jumped me.

But in the split second it took me to determine my next move, the door slightly moved like it hadn't fully latched when I'd left earlier.

Breathing a sigh of relief, I pushed open the door, ready to dart inside before anyone else saw me—that was, until I saw there was someone in my room. No, not someone—people.

As I stood before the open door in my underwear, blood trickling down my skin, three pairs of eyes stared back at me.

Guy O'Rourke.

Then the voluptuous brunette I'd been introduced to once in the cafeteria.

And Finley...

CHAPTER 16

I froze, not knowing what to do. As much as I wanted to attack, I was in no condition to remotely hold my own. The thought of running crossed my mind, but the fact that I was flaunting my ripped underwear gave me pause. So, in the end, all I could seem to do was stand there with the door open, giving the unwelcomed visitors one hell of a show.

Finley quickly diverted his gaze, then turned his body away from me. Guy's eyes ran the full length of my body, surprised, but he almost seemed concerned by my condition. And Big Boobs smirked like this was all a big joke.

"If you guys are here to kill me, then just get it over with because I've had an absolutely shitty day and I'm utterly fucking exhausted," I said, trying to get a gauge on how much trouble I was really in.

"No one's here to harm you whatsoever, let alone kill you," Guy said, finally lifting his eyes to meet mine.

"Props, girl," Big Boobs said. "Just walking around like that. Bold."

"That's me," I said. "Simply don't give a shit." I stepped into the room, letting the door close behind me. "Now, if you'll excuse me, I'd like to put some clothes on—you know, with my brother here and all."

"You look like you lost a fight with a cat—a big cat."

"I wouldn't say I lost."

"By all means," Guy said, then turned as well, presumably to give me a smidgen of privacy.

My underwear was bloody and wet from the scrapes and crawling through the snow, but I wasn't about to change out of it with these three in the room, so I threw on a long-sleeved shirt and jeans from the dresser.

"Okay; so let's get to the bottom of what the hell you're doing in my room," I said once I was decent.

Guy turned back to me. Big Boobs had never repositioned herself, though her attention was more distracted with checking out the room than me. But Finley remained with his back to me.

"I thought this was Fin's room," Guy said. "I see his stuff's still here."

I cringed at the sound of my brother being called

Fin. It still irritated me to no end. "Yeah; well, since he left, they gave it to me."

"What happened to that antsy kid?" Big Boobs asked.

"He dropped out. He wasn't cut out for this shit," I said.

"Maeve, in case you don't remember, this is Lisbon," Guy said, gesturing to Big Boobs.

"I remember," I lied, crossing my arms over my chest. My bra was so cold under my shirt. "And you still haven't answered my question. Why the hell are you here?"

"I never wanted to see any harm done to your brother," Guy said, cryptically. "And I know what happened was hard and I regret everything went down the way it did."

"It's a little late for apologies. Your guys nearly killed Devon and me. That freak of a man *did* kill two angels. He ripped off their wings before throwing them from the tower! How much more barbaric can you get? Then my brother—the one person in the world I trusted more than anyone— steals my needle from me? I'm sure you guys had a hand in that, but... I can't even begin to explain the hurt that caused."

"I may have had a hand in that," Guy admitted. "I'll admit it. And Fin didn't take it lightly. I know he feels terrible, as do I for suggesting such a family betrayal. But we're at war, and during war, things that would normally be considered black and white become gray and murky. We may be on opposing sides, but we're not the bad guys—at least not all of us."

"Are you saying *we're* the bad guys?" I asked, incredulously.

"I'm not saying that, either. Though no one in this fight is completely clean."

"Guy, we need to go," Lisbon said. "With the condition she's in, there could be someone coming to check on her at any moment."

"You're right," Guy said, making a move for the door.

"No one's coming for me," I said, taking a side-step to block the door. "So, how about some goddamn answers."

"This is the safest place for him. I did what I could. You need to watch over him now," Guy said, stopping in front of me. "He'll have to tell you the rest."

Before I could inquire further, Guy and Lisbon pushed past me and rushed out of the room. My attempt to stop them was weak, and when I stepped into the hallway, they were already gone.

My head swimming with anger and confusion, I marched back into the room. "Okay, little man. You better start talking!" I demanded. I was in no mood for more cryptic explanations. I wanted to know exactly what was going on right the hell now.

Finley still refused to look at me, his body remaining pointed toward the back of the room. I dropped a hand on his shoulder and pulled him around, forcing him to face me. I needed him to look me in the eyes and explain why he'd betrayed me. But when I finally saw his face, an audible gasp escaped my lips—my irate expression morphing to horror.

Just like the monstrous man I'd seen in the tower, Finley's mouth was completely sewn shut with red thread. And I had a pretty good idea where that thread had come from. Finley gazed up at me with terrified eyes and tear-stricken cheeks.

"Holy shit!" I cried, then immediately pulled down the collar of his shirt. He didn't have the octagram tattoo, though I couldn't be certain he ever had it.

I remembered the monstrous man from the tower and that horrifying voice that rang out in my head when he spoke. I doubted Finley had that ability.

"Who did this to you?" I asked as overprotective concern returned for my little brother. I couldn't have fathomed the tables being turned on me so suddenly—*again*. "Let me try to cut you free."

However, Finley adamantly shook his head to that suggestion. I went for my toiletry bag anyway to retrieve a small pair of scissors.

"Don't move," I said as I slipped one blade of the

scissors through a red strand. "I don't want to cut you." The thread was pulled tight, but I was able to push some of his skin aside to fully slip the blade through. Then I squeezed the handles, expecting the thread to split, allowing me to then pull it out.

But the thread wouldn't split. I pushed the scissor blade in deeper to get more leverage. I squeezed as hard as I could, so much so that Finley cringed from the pressure. If I slipped, I'd send that blade straight through his lips, which I really didn't want to do. But no matter how hard I tried, I couldn't cut the thread. I couldn't make so much as a fray or a kink in it. I might as well be trying to cut steel with plastic scissors.

With a frustrated sigh, I carefully removed the scissors from Finley's lips and tossed them onto my bed.

"Can you speak at all?" I asked.

His mouth moved, but his lips wouldn't part a single millimeter. I could hear a faint groan coming from inside his mouth, but nothing more. Then Finley sadly shook his head.

Despite the setback, I was still determined to get answers. I rushed over to what used to be Grayson's desk and rummaged through the drawers. I found a used spiral notebook and quickly flipped to an empty page. Then I grabbed a pen from a plastic cup atop the desk and handed it to Finley.

"What the hell happened to you? Why did Guy

bring you back?" I asked and slid the notebook closer to him, demanding answers.

The terror didn't leave Finley's eyes as he took the pen and notebook. He brought the pen to paper and started to write—or attempted to write, more like it. Or fought some strange urge not to write. I couldn't be sure. All I knew was what I saw—and that was Finley trying to form a letter, then frantically scribbling nonsense across the page.

"What are you doing?" I asked.

Finley repositioned the pen at a clean spot on the paper and started again. The result was no clearer. It was simply a preschooler's abstract scribbling. His eyes welled up again and tears spilled down his cheeks as he let the pen drop to the floor.

I reached over to take the notebook when he crushed me with a desperate hug, his whole body now racked with sobs. I didn't know how I felt about the surprising situation and it took me a few moments before returning his embrace.

Then I suddenly saw the boy in my room as my little brother again—weak, scared, and dependent—and all the fury and resentment that had consumed me since our last encounter steadily melted away.

CHAPTER 17

*W*ell, the plan of searching for Finley was no longer needed. He didn't have the crystals of our parents, but I should have expected that. I guess it was too much to ask for to get everything back at once. And I didn't even get a chance to ask him about the vial of my blood floating around Kicryria somewhere.

Now I just needed to figure out what to do with Finley, and I started by enlisting Devon for help—just so long as he promised not to tell anyone. He did and came to check out Finley for himself.

It turned out that the only way to cut a seamstress's thread was with her own needle. Another needle wouldn't do, so the headmistress wouldn't be any help. And unless Finley had done this to himself, the situation also seemed to suggest he no longer had my needle.

Guy had brought him here and told me to keep him safe, meaning he was in some sort of danger. I didn't know what that meant, and Finley obviously wasn't spilling the beans.

Who the hell has my needle now? Where were my parents' crystals? Who were my parents? Where was my freakin' blood? And what was the purpose for it in the first place?

I had so many questions swirling around in my mind, I thought my damn head might explode.

Then there was the practical issue of Finley's mouth being sewn shut. The thread was more than just thread, but a magical binding. It could not be cut, and it could not be spread apart. Finley's lips were not merely sewn together, but essentially glued shut. This made breathing more dangerous and the processes of eating and drinking far more difficult.

Devon quickly worked to master a new ability that I wasn't ready to even attempt yet. We were trying to keep the professors out of the picture because I didn't want Finley taken away from me. I needed to look after him, like I always had. I had vegetable smoothies and protein shakes made in the cafeteria and brought back to the room for Finley. And Devon perfected the magical art of puncturing Finley's cheek with the straw, so he could ingest the food semi-normally. As hard as it was for me to watch, it sounded way better than alternatives I researched that were used in hospitals and seemed far more invasive.

Finley whimpered like a beaten puppy the first few times, but he either got used to the procedure or Devon got better at it.

The next issue was keeping Finley hidden within the dorm. The only time he left the room was to use the bathroom. Devon secured a makeshift bedpan—actually, a real pot from the cafeteria—for Finley to use during the day, when he could be easily spotted. During the middle of the night, he'd be much less likely to run into someone else, so that's when I arranged for him to use the first-floor bathroom to do his business and take quick showers.

After a week, we were falling into a strange routine and Finley had so far remained undetected. Since I had to get a new coat and boots, I bought him a hooded winter coat too, and once the sun went down, we took the occasional walk in the dark. I did not permit him to venture out alone—and he was so nervous and broken that he made no attempts to try.

I couldn't believe I'd lost my damn Docs and leather jacket. Spellcrest Village didn't have good replacements—at least, not per my taste.

Then there was the issue of my phone. Ultimately, I told all my friends I'd lost it—even Devon—and simply got a new one. I didn't tell anyone about the attack and no one had fessed up to the topiary catching fire. That wizard was all burned to hell.

Well… I told Finley about all of it because I needed to tell *someone*, but it wasn't like he was going to gossip about it. I didn't want anyone fighting my battles for me, especially Devon. And those Master Classmen assholes were going to pay me back one way or another. That was a promise.

Professor Windsor had also taken me aside after one class to tell me the protective spell request had been approved and she cast it on me as soon as all the students had exited the classroom. I had no idea what it would actually do—if anything at all. But at least it would help me sleep a little better at night believing that the Kicryrians with my blood wouldn't be able to take advantage of me, at least not within the confines of the Academy.

Even though I no longer needed to find Finley, the basic plan Razielle, Nym, and I hatched out over break was still needed and more imperative than ever. I had to get my needle back to free Finley, find my parents' crystals, get some answers, and regain my magical strength. The protective spell probably wouldn't extend that far, but it was a chance I knew I had to take.

A part of me wanted to bring Finley with us, to act as our guide instead of us wandering around aimlessly in Kicryria, but Guy's warning rang loudly in my head. I wasn't sure what I was going to do.

. . .

"Hold still, will you?" Devon said, exasperated. He was trying to bring the straw for the fruit and vegetable smoothie to Finley's cheek, but Finley wasn't having it. "You need to eat!"

Finley defiantly shook his head, then dropped back onto his bed, rolling away from us to face the wall.

"Maeve, tell him he has to eat. We need to get to class."

"If he's not hungry, then he's not hungry," I said, taking a seat on Finley's bed and placing a gentle hand on his side. "Are you good until lunch?"

He moved his head slightly, which I interpreted to be a nod.

"Okay, then," I said and snatched the smoothie out of Devon's hand and started to sip from the straw. "I don't want it to go to waste. Finley, I'll be back at lunchtime to check on you."

No reply. But that was already commonplace. If I'd thought Finley had been becoming depressed before when he was feeling inadequate, he was downright doom and gloom now. He obviously wasn't taking well to his magical punishment and it wasn't like I could reason with him. I just needed to keep him from doing anything stupid.

I donned my new winter coat and left the room with Devon.

"I don't know how much longer we can get away with hiding him," Devon said.

"It's worked so far," I said. "We just need to stay vigilant."

"Yeah…"

"Any sign of our friend?" I'd told Devon that Guy had brought back Finley, but I hadn't mentioned anything about Lisbon. I figured she'd still be around and I'd maybe have a chance to get something out of her. I didn't want her to get kicked out—at least, not yet. Unfortunately, so far, I hadn't been able to locate her.

"No," Devon said. "He's a ghost in a snowstorm. But I'll keep looking." When we reached the Windsor Hall entry, he stopped and kissed me. "I've got to run."

"I know," I said. "Nym should be here any moment. That little elf is never late."

Devon left me with one more kiss before running out the front door and into heavily falling snow.

There was a constant flux of students headed to class at this early morning hour, and Nym and Razielle were among them not two minutes later.

"Rise and dine, sunshines!" I exclaimed as they reached the bottom of the stairs.

"I wish I could have one of Elora's delicious breakfasts this morning instead of the power bar I just scarfed down," Razielle whined. "You did it— now I'm hungry again."

I still had half a smoothie in one hand and offered it to her. "You can finish this if you want."

She gladly took it from me until I added, "I didn't spit in it or anything."

Immediately, Razielle handed the plastic cup back to me, her face puckering up like she'd just sucked on a lemon.

"I'm kidding," I said, but she wouldn't take it back. I held it out to Nym and she also declined. "I'm not diseased or anything. Does your kind even get sick?"

"I'm not immune to getting sick," Nym said. "But I don't get sick often."

"Lucky you," I said as we headed out into the cold.

"I don't get sick," Razielle said. "It's not a Nephilim thing because my brothers do sometimes —it's just a me thing. Or maybe they're the special ones; I dunno. I just don't want your cootie-ridden smoothie." Then she laughed and purposefully bumped into me.

"How's your brother doing?" Nym asked.

"Not good, I'm afraid," I said. "It's time to finalize our plan and get the supplies we need to get to Kicryria." I'd told them about Finley's mouth being sewn shut, but they hadn't seen him for themselves. He was a secret I couldn't keep from my two best friends, but I still wanted to be careful.

"Are you sure we shouldn't enlist more help?" Nym asked, always the cautious and practical thinker.

"We can't risk being shut down," I said. "And I don't want to risk losing my brother again. We have to keep this quiet—and quiet requires a small team."

"But what about Devon? He's not a professor, but he's powerful and could be helpful."

"I trust him a lot," I said. "But I don't know exactly where his threshold lies with his duty to his mother and the Academy. It's too risky."

"Us going it alone is too risky."

"I told you from the beginning, you don't have to come," I said, wanting to raise my voice, but remaining conscious of the other students as we continued our walk to the Manor for Morality of Magic.

"Maybe this is a dilemma you should bring up in class," Razielle said, sounding almost serious.

"I'm not gonna ditch you guys," Nym said.

"How about we focus on getting what we need— the dagger and the totem—then we can revisit the idea of enlisting Devon," I said as a compromise. "We can focus on one step at a time."

"Sounds good to me," Razielle said, followed by a nod from Nym.

There—we had a plan. The biggest thing I needed their help with was locating and retrieving the dagger. If need be, I was confident I could take care of the rest on my own.

CHAPTER 18

*A*t lunch, Razielle, Nym, and I finished our food early, then left the rest of the group in the cafeteria. We had to search out Professor Voltaire, who taught the master class of Transfiguration. It was an introductory class of changing your appearance and more. Master Classmen were given a glimpse into transporting to emphasize the importance of blending into your surroundings for wherever—and *whenever*—you traveled to.

Students got a taste of traveling back in time, though it was only a few days or weeks, so there weren't any major disrupters. This was made possible by way of a specially enchanted artifact—a dagger with an infused seamstress needle that could cut through space and time. As one could expect— like the existence of seamstresses themselves—an artifact of this ability was extremely rare.

I didn't have any illusions that it wouldn't be well guarded. We first needed to find out what kind of protections we were dealing with. Then we'd have to figure out how to get past them.

I imagined the totem would be easier to acquire. I just needed to know when the headmistress was away on business again, which seemed to be rather often.

Razielle had been given Professor Voltaire's office number from Arius, so we headed up to the third floor and found him sitting at his desk, grading papers. He was a younger man than I was expecting, though I guessed appearances could be deceiving—especially in *his* specialty. He was a handsome-looking man, seemingly well-built and somewhere in his thirties. He wore a fitted dress shirt with the collar open and his crystal tucked inside. He had a thick and shiny head of hair any man would be proud of, and obviously took great care in keeping it groomed.

Razielle rapped on the glass within the office door, at which he immediately glanced up and waved us in.

"May I help you, ladies?" he asked, in a baritone voice as smooth and silky as his hair.

Razielle took the lead, heading straight to his desk. "My name is Razielle Valentine. You had my brother Arius in one of your classes last year."

"Yes; a smart boy," he said with a smile. "And

there was another one in your family a few years earlier." He chewed on his cheek as he tried to recall a name.

"Oren," Razielle said.

"That's it. He had some real natural talent."

"Yes; he's my parents' golden boy," she said, not sounding bitter whatsoever. "I'm the black sheep of the family."

Professor Voltaire didn't nod in agreement, but he sized her up by her hard appearance and less-than-approachable style, and didn't seem to object to the notion. "We all have our strengths and weaknesses," he said after a moment's pause. "So, what can I do for you?"

While Razielle was holding the professor's attention, I was checking out the room, taking stock of whatever I could. Nym was doing the same, and we'd have to compare mental notes afterward.

There were a lot of strange and beautiful artifacts and pictures decorating his wall. Some looked like they spanned the globe, some like they were absolutely ancient, while some looked altogether other-worldly. His office resembled a natural history museum. A glass case of pinned insects—from tiny to skin-crawlingly monstrous—hung from one wall. Some kind of long-beaked bird mask hung from another. The wall directly behind him had a rack of different-styled swords. And as I craned my neck upward, locked away in another glass case above the swords hung an ornately-forged dagger.

That had to be the one. It couldn't be this easy.

"Arius was talking about this class over break and how awesome it was," Razielle said. "You were his favorite professor. So, he thought I should swing by and introduce myself, even though I won't be in your class for another three years."

"I appreciate that," Professor Voltaire said, beaming. "And the time does go by quickly. It feels like just yesterday that Oren was in my class. You'll be a Master Classman, too, before you know it." Then he glanced over at me. "Aren't you the girl in the crypt last trimester—during the attack." He sat up straighter in his desk chair.

"You got me," I said, only now realizing he had been one of the professors chasing down Guy, Otis, and the others. There were several professors I hadn't recognized and hadn't paid much attention to. "Not one of my better nights."

He looked empathetic and wanted to hear more of the story leading up to that unfortunate climax, so I gave him the short version—one that didn't include my brother betraying me, but simply nefarious Kicryrians arriving in the lonely tower and later stealing my needle. Now, it was kind of true.

"That was the first infiltration onto campus in a long time," Professor Voltaire said, his eyes sad. "It was hard to learn about how vulnerable we still were. I'm sorry about the loss of your needle, but glad you're ultimately okay and still in the Academy."

"Thank you," I said with a smile.

"What about you, young lady?" he asked, now turning his gaze to Nym. "What's your story?"

Nym looked as nervous as being called on in class. "I—I don't have a story. I'm just here."

"Everyone has a story," Professor Voltaire said with a hearty chuckle. "Everyone who attends Spell-crest is exceptional in one way or another."

"I'm not saying I don't like who I am... I... umm... just don't feel like I have an exceptional story."

"So, you do admit you have a story?" The professor steepled his fingers on his desk, giving her a sly smile.

I actually didn't know a whole lot about her childhood because she rarely talked about herself, so I was interested to hear more too. But in typical Nym style, she got in her own head and gave a meek shrug.

"I don't know," she finally said.

I jabbed her in the side, hoping to give her the small push she needed, but it didn't work. Nym clammed up tight.

Professor Voltaire finally took pity on her. "Well, you have time to think about it—two and a half years to be exact. But when you reach my class, I'll be expecting you to share."

Nym nodded then sank behind me like a young child.

"Well, we don't want to take up too much of your lunch hour," Razielle said. "It was nice to meet you."

"Likewise," Professor Voltaire said, giving us a polite wave, then returning to grading papers as we exited the room.

Once we were out in the hallway with the door closed behind us, Razielle elbowed me in the arm. "Did you see it?"

"How could you not," I said. "It was blatantly out on display. I thought it would have been hidden, under lock and key."

"I don't want to take his class," Nym whined. "He's going to pick on me—I can tell."

"He's not going to pick on you," I assured her. "He just wants to help you out of your shell, as we all do."

"And that's like years away," Razielle said. "Calm down. We've got plenty more to worry about right now. Like, how are we gonna get the knife?"

"You were the one with the plan," I said as we made our way to the stairs.

"Yeah, I had the plan of getting us in there to look around, and I did that. Now, it's your turn to step up."

"I'll think of something," I said and started down

the stairs ahead of them, already racking my brain for our next step. If I'd still had my needle, then this would be easy. Then again, if I'd still had my needle, we wouldn't need the dagger. I needed to find a way that wouldn't get us instantly busted.

CHAPTER 19

"*J*ust ask Devon to help us," Razielle said.

We were stationed by one of the benches off a main sidewalk on the Academy grounds after getting out of Combative Casting. Nym palmed some snow off the bench to sit down. I preferred to stand.

Another week had passed, and we were no closer to getting the dagger because I had no plausible plan. I didn't want to just break into Professor Voltaire's office, smash the glass case, and make a run for it like a common criminal. There had to be a better way to retrieve the dagger. However, a part of me wondered if it really mattered, since the dagger was on full display in the office. It going missing from the case wouldn't pass unnoticed for long.

But I wasn't willing to give up.

"No," I said. "I'm not willing to chance that yet."

"I'd think your brother's going crazy by this point," Razielle said.

"He's made his bed, so he'll have to lie in it for as long as it takes." I crossed my arms, not as an act of defiance, but just trying to stay warm. The sun was out and there wasn't much wind this afternoon, but the calm air was still icy cold.

"Do you have *any* ideas?" Nym asked.

"Besides what we've already talked about? No; I've got nothing. But that doesn't mean it's time to quit, but to think harder." I missed my crystal—the small comfort and warmth Eileen had brought. I was suffering more in Combative Casting despite my extra practicing. The crystal did provide a noticeable difference. And unless I was willing to get my ass kicked in my underwear in sub-zero temperatures on a regular basis—to harness enough rage to accomplish menial magical feats—then I needed another one.

"What are you guys talking about?" Ivanic asked, crunching toward us through the snow. Bree was at his side, a purple scarf pulled tight around her neck.

"Maeve had a rough casting class, that's all," Razielle said.

"Maeve's had a rough few months—what else is new?" Ivanic retorted, placing a hand on my shoulder.

"I'm not complaining about it, but just trying to move forward," I said. They didn't know about my brother being back, and I still didn't want to share that monumental bit of information. Luckily, Ivanic hadn't randomly shown up at my room. With Devon back in the picture, he was keeping a bit more distance, though his verbal advances never ceased.

"She needs her crystal back," Nym said.

"It seems so unlike you to lose things—especially something so important," Bree said.

"Not to mention her phone," Razielle said.

"Haven't you lost or broken three phones so far this year?" Nym asked.

"We're not talking about me," Razielle snapped back. "And that third time was not my fault at all. You try not to drop your phone while a bird dive-bombs at you in mid-flight."

"Why did you even have your phone out while you were flying?" Ivanic asked.

"I got a text," Razielle said, hands on her hips. "I had to know what it said."

"I don't think it's wise to text and fly," I said, a laugh escaping my lips just trying to picture the incident.

"It's not like there are many obstacles up there," Razielle said, exasperated.

"Except birds, apparently," Bree said.

"And other angels," I added. "Also, besides you losing your phone, you could have killed someone. Ever think of that?"

Razielle was quiet for a moment, seeming to really consider my statement. "No... I hadn't."

I happened to glance past our group at other students walking along the sidewalks, when something caught my attention. There was a girl walking alone with a long black winter coat and a fur-trimmed hood pulled tightly over her head. But when my gaze dropped to her feet, I noticed her boots... Docs... Docs with very distinct scuff and scratch patterns...

I didn't say anything to my friends, but immediately pushed past Ivanic and Bree. "Hey!" I shouted as I marched toward the girl who now had her back to me. "Those are *my* boots!"

"What?" Ivanic asked the others as I bolted away from the group.

The girl glanced back from the sound of me yelling at her. When she saw it was just me, she stopped and turned to face me, seemingly unintimidated. Wavy red hair spilled from the sides of her furry hood.

I couldn't be sure she was one of the girls who'd been there to torture me that evening until she opened her mouth. "You just don't learn, do you?" she said. "You're as stubborn as you are stupid."

"And you should know better than to screw with stubborn people," I said, stopping a few feet from her. "We just keep coming."

"Then I guess we didn't do a good job of finishing you off last time, normy."

"Where's the rest of my stuff?" I demanded, just as the cavalry arrived, filling the space behind me.

"What's going on?" Razielle asked.

"Now you want to be humiliated in front of your friends?" the girl asked, her gaze still trained on me.

"There's five of us and one of you," Razielle said.

"Five neophytes can't handle one Master Classman," the girl said with a laugh. "Why don't you all run along before someone gets hurt."

I knew she was stalling, trying to intimidate us since she didn't want to attack in broad daylight. There were a lot of witnesses here, as well as professors out and about, making it much harder to sneak away from a public encounter.

On the other hand, I didn't give a shit about getting caught fighting with a girl who'd stolen one of my most prized possessions—and could most likely lead me to the other things I'd thought were gone for good.

"Then just give me back my Docs and we can be square," I said, knowing full well she wouldn't go for it.

The girl laughed again. "And why would I do that?"

"Because I'm not backing down. You can do whatever to me right here in front of everyone and you're gonna get nailed for it. You give me back my Docs and I'll walk away without reporting you for what you and your friends did to me." My friends hadn't heard the story, and I could hear whispers of curiosity coming from behind me. When I glanced back, I noticed Bree and Razielle both had their cellphones out, recording the confrontation. That made me smile, and I turned back to the redhead with more confidence.

"I'm live streaming, so don't even think about doing anything to my phone," Razielle warned.

"Fine," the girl sighed. "But you better give me *your* boots."

"Sure thing," I said. "But hand my Docs over first."

"No way. Same time." She bent down to untie the boots but kept them on.

A few other students had stopped to watch at this point. With the camera phones up, it made it look like something was going down. Then I saw other phones out too. This girl wouldn't be able to destroy all the evidence.

I unlaced my winter boots and slipped them off my feet, forcing me to stand on the freezing side-walk in my socks—which was still way warmer than it had been when this girl and her friends had attacked me. I held out the boots, letting them dangle from one hand.

"Your turn," I said.

The girl slipped off my Docs and held them out

too, and we each snatched the other's boots. She immediately knelt to put them on to keep her feet from freezing, but I already knew what my body could endure.

I tossed my Docs behind me, toward my closely gathered group of friends, then dove at the girl while she was off balance. Our bodies collided, and I elbowed her in the face as we both went down.

The girl grunted and cried out just before the back of her head bounced off the sidewalk with a nauseating thud. In one move, I essentially robbed her of all her magical abilities. There was no way she was going to regain focus or concentration anytime soon.

There were also gasps from the growing crowd of spectators, by whom I was sure there were more recordings being made, but I wasn't going to worry about that now.

I was able to retain control during the fall and quickly startled her, getting into position to really let her have it and demand the rest of my stuff, when I noticed she was already out cold.

Shit...

How could she give me any information if she was unconscious? That sure had backfired. I wanted to punch her once just for aggravating me more by passing out, when I heard an all-too-familiar voice— one that made me cringe.

"What is the meaning of this?" Headmistress

Christi demanded. "Maeve, get off Alexi this instant!"

"Yes, ma'am," I said, scrambling off the redhead and going for my Docs, which Nym was now holding.

While I laced up my boots, the headmistress knelt beside Alexi and put a hand to the unconscious girl's head. Within seconds, Alexi stirred, shaking her head like she'd been given smelling salt. Her eyes shot open and her gaze darted nervously around as she tried to make sense of what had happened. When she saw the headmistress leaning over her fallen body, her eyes went wide.

"Headmistress Christi, am I okay?" she whimpered, still seemingly unsure of what was going on.

"You're fine, dear. But I would like a word with you and Ms. Rhodes in my office." The headmistress stood and offered Alexi a hand. "Everyone, go about your business. I'm sure you all have classes to get to."

I'd never seen students scatter so fast. And my friends weren't far behind.

"Good luck," Razielle said, her tone exuding empathy. No doubt she'd been to the principal's office numerous times in her previous schools. But so had I.

"I'll say she hit you first," Ivanic said.

"Don't worry about me," I said, giving him a warm smile. "I can handle this. If you could, just tell Devon I'll probably be late."

"I'll make sure he doesn't lock you out again."

I had to laugh at that comment, thinking back to how far we'd come and how much had changed since the beginning of last trimester. And here I was getting in trouble, which I said I wouldn't do—and by his own mother, no less.

I just couldn't seem to help myself.

CHAPTER 20

$\mathcal{H}$eadmistress Christi's office was just as I'd remembered it—invisible walls and all—and much like our trip to Professor Voltaire's office, I glanced around for the important item I needed. My eyes leveled on the ornate chess board and I easily picked out the queen Devon had placed in my hand. The pieces weren't matching, so I identified it almost immediately.

"What do you girls have to say for yourselves?" the headmistress asked with an overly amplified authoritative tone. She'd sat us side by side on one of the couches. "This doesn't have anything to do with the fire on the first day of class, does it?"

I turned my head to Alexi, curious to see if she'd go first. It was clear she was considering her options.

When Alexi didn't offer an explanation right away and it was clear I wasn't going to fully incriminate myself, the headmistress came to stand before our couch, positioned directly between us. She bent down and took one of our wrists in each of her hands.

"Did one of you cause the fire?" she asked.

"Yes," I blurted out, without taking even a moment to think—or I wasn't allowed to think. It felt like I couldn't withhold the answer to the question.

"I suspected as much, but I'm willing to venture there was a defensive reason," the headmistress said, turning her head to Alexi.

"A group of my friends stole her crystal, and when she tried to get it back, we stole her clothes to teach her a lesson," Alexi said.

I could tell by the look on her face that she didn't want to be spilling the information, but like me, she seemed compelled to answer.

"And what lesson would that be?"

"That she's a neophyte and needs to learn her place. She isn't special."

I shouldn't have been overly surprised when the headmistress smiled at this. "Because of the right to wear a crystal?"

"Yes."

"And how did the topiary get burned down?" the headmistress turned her attention back to me.

"I was trying to signal someone for help. I was afraid I was going to freeze to death," I said. I didn't need to feel compelled to keep talking, even though I still felt the nudge.

"You weren't going to freeze to death," Alexi said, which caught me by surprise.

"How do you figure?" I argued. "I was locked inside a freakin' bush with no clothes on."

"You still had your underwear—and a protective spell keeping you minimally warm. Your body was protected from the elements as much as if you still had your outerwear. The fear of freezing was all in your mind."

"This wasn't all in my mind," I snapped back, lifting my shirt to expose my midsection and the crisscrossing scrapes that were still healing. "Nor was me almost being burned at the stake."

"That was your own fault," Alexi said.

With a chuckle, Headmistress Christi released us from her truthfulness hold and returned to a standing position.

It took me a moment for the information that Alexi had just dropped onto me to fully sink in. It had still been a prank. I hadn't been left out in the nighttime cold to die, even though it sure as hell had felt like it at the time.

"Maeve, you need to be careful with your fireworks," the headmistress said, taking a seat on the adjacent couch.

"Me? I'm the one in trouble here? You heard what they did to me."

"Yes, another immature prank on a first year. I know that you of all people can handle it. And the pair of you can spend your weekend doing community service. I'll have Professor Voltaire make the arrangements and notify each of you with the details. Perhaps a little hard labor will make you think twice about fighting on school grounds. And if it doesn't… well, there's always more work to be done."

"I want the rest of my stuff back," I demanded. "The rest of my clothes, my phone, and my crystal."

"I'm revoking your use of crystals," the headmistress said. "It seems to be causing too much trouble." She turned her gaze to Alexi. "Bring me her crystal today and return the rest of her personal effects on Saturday."

"And what about the others in her group who jumped me?" I asked, my voice laced with disdain at the headmistress's decision to no longer allow me to use a soul crystal.

"You will get your things back and this representative of the group who harassed you is being punished," the headmistress said, casually. "Don't push your luck."

"I don't know who has her phone," Alexi said.

"Then find out and make sure it's returned," Headmistress Christi said. "If everything's not returned on Saturday, then Professor Voltaire will inform me and there will be a bigger price to pay than one weekend of work."

"Yes, Headmistress. I'll make sure I gather up everything that was taken."

"I have no doubt, and you are excused." The headmistress nodded to Alexi, who quickly stood and scampered from the office.

"Why does it seem like I'm in more trouble when it was her and her friends who attacked *me*?" I asked, my eyes narrowed at her.

"I found you fighting with her in front of a large body of students. That behavior cannot go unpunished."

"Fine," I said. "What about taking my crystal privileges away?"

"As you said, it is a privilege—one you no longer deserve. If you want the privilege back, then you will have to earn it."

"And how can I do that?"

"For starters, stay out of trouble. Stop bringing so much negative attention toward yourself. Do as you're told. This trimester is off to a rocky start, but we'll see how it ends. If all goes well, perhaps I'll allow you to have a new one next trimester."

"What will we be doing on Saturday?" I asked, knowing I wasn't getting anywhere with the crystal request. By the time the next trimester rolled around, I was sure she'd have found a new reason not to give me one.

"It will have to be discussed," she said, waving me off. "You'll be informed of your assignment on Saturday morning."

"Can't wait," I said, sarcastically—earning me a disapproving glare from the headmistress. "Is there anything else you want to discuss?"

"Have you heard from your brother yet? He is the one who took your needle, was he not? Your neophyte little brother?" Headmistress Christi asked, really emphasizing that last part.

"He had help," I clarified, making sure she understood I could defend myself against my little brother. At this point, I wasn't surprised she knew. "And no, I have not heard from him."

"But you would tell me if you did."

"Of course," I said, hoping to God she didn't grab my wrist again to perform her magical lie-detector test.

"It's very important we get that needle back. I can't stress that enough. We are vulnerable without it, and it's my job to ensure the situation is remedied."

"I understand." I shifted uncomfortably on the couch. "Please tell me something about my parents. You said you weren't surprised I could still see the seam in my apartment because of my father. What did that mean? Who was he? Who was my mother? I thought I knew them both. I thought we were a normal, happy family before they were killed. Now

I realize everything I thought I knew can't be trusted."

Headmistress Christi was quiet for a long time, carefully considering what she wanted to tell me. When she finally spoke, my heart leapt into my throat, desperate to know what she was going to reveal—if anything at all.

"I wouldn't say I knew them, although I knew *of* them," she started. "Your father was a lieutenant in the Kicryrian army and your mother was from here —Earth. I know nothing about your early family life, and with your father being who he was, I'm surprised you weren't introduced to magic at a young age. But that's neither here nor there. Kicryrians are naturally more in tune with their abilities than humans. Since you have Kicryrian blood, your abilities should come to you easier than most. Your needle was not supplying you with all or most of your power. However, that would typically go for anyone."

The small detail of my father actually being a Kicryrian was world-shattering, except there wasn't much left of my world to shatter. Most of it was shards littering the ground around my feet.

I just didn't understand how this war and my family life fit together. He worked for a disaster relief non-profit and would have to travel periodically for work, but it wasn't like he was gone all the time. He was usually home for dinner and we had family outings on weekends. I didn't understand when he could be out fighting a war.

"How did they die?" I asked, feeling a lump growing in the back of my throat. "I'm assuming it wasn't from a random mugging as I'd been told."

"They were posted outside a portal in Southern California—tasked with holding it open to move people and supplies between the two worlds. Your father was able to mostly mask the detectability of the portal. It had gone unnoticed for a long time. But the spell eventually went down, putting the seam on our radar. Helena was the one to notice it first. She was also the first to observe the operation and request reinforcements to shut it down. Your parents were casualties of that fight."

"Did you…" I couldn't get the words out to finish my sentence.

"No," she said. "I wasn't there for that fight. I'm not even sure who officially extracted them. But it is a general practice for those types of fights. And not just us. The Kicryrians do the same thing. In fact, it was a practice we learned from *them*. We've grown that much stronger because of it.

"I know this doesn't answer all your questions, but hopefully it gives you a little something. If Helena were still here, she'd be able to tell you more since she was there."

"Did she know? Did she know who I was when she chose me?"

Headmistress Christi shrugged. "I can only assume, but it also makes for a great coincidence."

I had to believe that she did. If only she were still here to answer my questions—give me more insight to who my parents really were and what their last moments were like. Though maybe it was better that I didn't know the specific way in which they'd died. At least I knew they weren't shot in a random mugging. They were killed doing something they believed in—something they were willing to give their lives for—even at the expense of their children.

I felt tears stinging the corners of my eyes but pinched the bridge of my nose like it was merely allergies. "How did it go from them being killed in a magical battle to me being told they were killed in a mugging?"

"The fewer missing persons the better. It's better to create a backstory to someone's death than have them simply disappear. Closure is important—for surviving family members and investigative services. Most of the people in these fights are Kicryrian, people with no records on Earth, so coverups aren't necessary. For your parents, a cleaning crew was dispatched. Your father may have been a Kicryrian lieutenant, but like some Kicryrians infiltrating our planet, he assumed the identity of an American citizen and was legally married to your mother. We thought it important to explain his death as well." She stopped and looked at me. "Are you okay?"

"Fine," I said, my nose running now, but I held back the sobs. I didn't know how I'd react to receiving this information, even though much of it wasn't overly specific. But it had to do with my parents, whom I'd always miss dearly. True, they had lied to my brother and me—but we were also young and wouldn't have truly understood anyway. I was confident they would have told us as we grew older —if only they'd gotten the chance to.

I wanted to know more about this cause they had fought and died for, but it was the primary opposing force to what I was being currently taught, directed by the woman sitting across from me. I wouldn't get an unbiased explanation of what the Kicryrians truly wanted with our world in this office. For that, I'd have to venture into enemy territory, something I'd been preparing myself for since returning to the Academy.

CHAPTER 21

*S*even o'clock in the morning was too damn early for a Saturday. Apparently, most of the people in Spellcrest Village thought so too because the village was practically empty.

I met Professor Voltaire and Alexi in the village square. I couldn't talk Nym out of coming with me. She was prepared to help in whatever way the professor allowed. On the other hand, Razielle said she wanted to be supportive, but she wasn't getting up at the butt crack of dawn on a Saturday. I could relate to her aversion to manual labor on a weekend morning. I certainly wasn't here by choice.

There was a beautiful stone fountain in the center of the square where the water shooting up in a brilliant formation had become a glistening ice sculpture. At its base was where I found the professor and Alexi. She was still wearing the boots I'd traded with her earlier in the week, and of course, I had on my Docs. On the ground beside her was a black trash bag.

"Where's my stuff?" I demanded as I approached with Nym at my side.

Alexi pointed apathetically to the bag by her feet.

"Good morning," Professor Voltaire said cheerfully. "Brought a cheerleader, I see."

"I'm here to work," Nym said, then added, "If that's okay."

"Your help won't allow your friend to get her work done faster, though I suppose no one will complain about *more* work being done. If you want to work, then you're welcome to stay."

I picked up the bag and rummaged inside. My leather jacket and what appeared to be the rest of my clothes were in there. As expected, the crystal was not. Then I found my phone and took it out of the bag. The glass screen had a spiderweb of cracks and the casing was severely dented, almost folded in half.

"What the hell is this?" I asked, holding up what was left of my phone.

"At least I found it, right?" Alexi said, a devious grin flirting with the edges of her lips. "That should be everything."

"Did you receive everything that was taken from you?" the professor asked.

"If you call this acceptable," I said, still holding up my phone, so he could get a good look.

"It was an accident," Alexi said.

"Sure, it was," I snapped.

"I believe that is salvageable," Professor Voltaire said. "I'll see if I can fix it."

"Work your magic," I said, handing over my old phone. The fact was, I didn't really care if it could be fixed or not at this point since I'd already gotten a replacement, transferred the number, and most of my pictures had been saved to the cloud. I just didn't want it floating around somewhere out of my control.

"I will," he said with a smile. "But you girls won't be working yours today." Then he eyed Nym. "Though you, my dear, can use whatever magic you like since you're a volunteer. Your name is Nym, right?"

Nym was still petrified of starting his class in two and a half years, and him remembering her name didn't help. Maybe I should have told her that he was the professor overseeing the community service this morning. Maybe I hadn't tried as hard to talk her out of coming as I'd let on.

Professor Voltaire led us over to one of the shops where there were two buckets of soapy water, squeegees, and rolls of paper towels. "Your first task will be cleaning the inside and outside of all the storefront windows in the square."

I gazed around at the surrounding shops, seeing just how much glass there was to clean. And there was a shitload.

"It snows practically every day," Alexi complained.

"The store owners still pride themselves on keeping their windows clean—inside and out," the professor said, handing her the first bucket. "And today, that job is yours—the old-fashioned way."

"Seems like a waste of time to me. It could be done like ten times faster with a little magic."

"That takes the fun and pride out of your work. There's something satisfying in physically working with your hands."

"There's nothing satisfying about being reduced to a Norm," Alexi whined.

"*No magic*," Professor Voltaire insisted, then handed the second bucket to me. "Sorry, Nym. I don't have a bucket prepared for you. I guess you can dry, or you can ask one of the clerks for another bucket of clean water."

"Nym can dry for me," I said. "We're a team."

Alexi scowled at us but didn't say anything.

"Very good," the professor said, then offered us business cards. "Give me a call when you're done, and I'll come back to inspect your work and instruct you on your next task."

"What? You're not staying out here with us?" Alexi asked.

Professor Voltaire laughed. "I'm not going to babysit you all day. But just because I'm not here doesn't mean you're not being watched. Every shop owner knows what you've been tasked with today and they will report to me if you're not performing your work as directed. No magic."

And with that, Professor Voltaire walked off, whistling to himself, headed back in the direction of the Academy.

I didn't want to spend my day next to Alexi—and it was obvious she felt the same way about me—so we split up, starting in different sections of the square. I carried my water bucket and paper towels while Nym hauled the trash bag of my meager belongings.

About half of the shops weren't even open yet, so we started at one that was. It was a small deli, and the curly-haired lady with dark blotches covering one side of her face was overly friendly. I set up my supplies on the inside, only having to drag one small table out of the way.

"Did you have breakfast?" Nym asked.

I shook my head. "I decided it was more important to sleep in."

"I'll get us some breakfast sandwiches. I'm sure you'll be allowed to eat."

"I can eat and work," I said and started wiping down the inside of the glass.

· · ·

THE MORNING WENT by quicker than I would have thought, and I didn't even see Alexi for most of it. She could have left for all I knew, but I wasn't going to put myself at risk of getting in more trouble. And besides, I had a friend by my side, so the tedious work wasn't so bad.

Razielle stopped by about midmorning. She hung out by the storefront we were working on and started talking, though she didn't offer to help once —not even to take Nym's place. However, by that time, it didn't matter. Nym and I had hit our stride and were in a good rhythm.

By lunchtime, Ivanic came down after receiving a call from Razielle. We all ordered lunch and sat outside to eat. I scarfed down my food and was cleaning another window before my friends were even halfway done.

In the section I was working on, there were only two shops left. On the opposite side of the square, I didn't know how far Alexi had gotten. I knew I'd have to reconvene with her sooner or later for an update.

"How long do you have to do this for?" Ivanic asked.

"I don't know," I said. "Until the professor tells me I'm done, I guess."

"What can I do to help?"

"I'm good. I've got Nym and that's all the help I need."

Ivanic's expression sank, but he nodded and walked back to where the others were still eating. Not thirty seconds later, he was back with a second wind. "I tagged Nym out," he said, a smile sneaking onto his face. "What would you have me do, boss?"

I glanced over my shoulder at Nym, who gave a sorrowful shrug like she felt guilty for giving her spot away. She had a hard time saying no to anyone.

"Wash or dry?" I asked.

"*Wash*," he answered, excitedly.

I handed him the dripping squeegee. "Go to town. I'll go next door and tell the shopkeeper we're coming."

"You better be back to dry. I'm not doing everything."

"If you want to retain Nym's position, then there shall be no backtalking. Got it?" I said in my best reprimanding tone.

"Yes, boss," Ivanic said, a smile still plastered across his face. "You know what would make this so much easier?"

"No magic!" I said just before entering the next shop.

A small bell sounded from the door opening. I glanced around the dimly-lit store, finding it empty of customers, but filled with exquisitely detailed wooden furniture, from rocking chairs to armoires, statues to picture frames.

Before I had a chance to explore, a tall older man

with deep wrinkles and white hair stepped out of a back room. "May I help you?" he asked in a kind, grandfatherly voice.

"My friend and I will be cleaning your windows. I just wanted to give you a head's up that we'll be starting soon. Do you mind if I move the items away from the windows?"

"Not at all," he said, already starting in that direction. "Allow me to help."

The only items that needed to be moved were two chairs and a small circular table with a chess set arranged atop it. The set reminded me of the one in Headmistress Christi's office, but even though her pieces were all wooden, they weren't matching since she collected them on her travels.

I thanked the shop clerk for his help and left with an idea. I headed straight for Nym and Razielle, who were now just sitting around and watching Ivanic work.

"These windows don't dry themselves," he called to me.

"I'll be right there," I answered, too focused on my new idea to come up with a witty remark. "Nym, can you do me a favor?"

"Sure," she said.

"In the shop I just came out of, there's a wooden chess set. Remember how I told you guys about the totem chess pieces the headmistress has?"

Both girls nodded.

"I need a queen," I said. "Can you get one for me? I don't want to raise any suspicion by buying it myself."

Nym agreed, and I went back to work.

CHAPTER 22

The shopkeeper told Nym that he wouldn't sell the chess pieces individually, that it could only be purchased as a set, and instead of haggling, she simply bought the whole set.

I should have expected that. And the whole set was $500—a little out of my price range—but to Nym, it was nothing. She might as well have been buying me a root beer.

Nym gave me the two queens and kept the rest of the set. It couldn't hurt to have a backup.

Professor Voltaire didn't deem us complete until 5 p.m., so needless to say, it was a long day. My arms were dead by that time. But to my surprise, he returned with my phone, which looked good as new. Maybe I shouldn't have been surprised. I thanked him, then gave Alexi a smug smile.

Take that, bitch.

I picked up dinner with my friends in the square before the restaurants filled, then the four of us headed back, me hauling a trash bag over one shoulder. I was beat and told the others I was calling it an evening.

Finley was lying on his bed when I arrived. He didn't do much anymore, and it showed. Between his stagnant lifestyle and how little he was eating, he was wasting away. He already lost a lot of weight in the past few weeks, and he didn't start out with much to lose.

"You hungry?" I asked.

He simply gazed over at me with hollow eyes without gesturing an answer.

"Did Devon stop in on you today?" I asked next. I'd asked him to since I had no idea how long my *community service* would last.

To this question, he gave a slight nod.

I was sure Devon would have force fed him no matter what, so I didn't bother to ask about it.

By my desk, there was a half empty case of bottled waters, and beside it, a large protein powder smoothie canister. On the desk was the shaker to make Finley's smoothies. Devon had brought the supplies, so I didn't always have to rely on getting a smoothie from the cafeteria.

Over the past few days, I'd even learned to feed Finley myself. I hadn't yet perfected the magical art of slipping the straw seamlessly through his cheek, but at least we—as a team—were becoming self-sufficient again.

Even though Finley gave no indication that he was hungry, I started fixing him a smoothie anyway.

"Sit up," I said, bringing the smoothie to his bed. "You have to eat."

He made no attempt to follow my orders.

"I don't want you to choke on it, but you're not going to stop me from feeding you. Sit up."

This time, he apathetically pushed up to a seated position, shook his head at me again, then looked away.

I wasn't deterred and brought the straw to his cheek. I harnessed the focus I'd been working on with Devon and pushed the straw into his skin. At first, it didn't feel like it was going to give. The straw was about to bend. But I didn't allow the pushback to impact my focus, and soon it slipped right through his flesh without much effort.

Finley let it sit in his mouth for a moment, almost challenging me that he still didn't have to eat, before starting to suck on the straw and drink the smoothie.

"I'm closer to getting you better," I whispered as I sat beside him while he continued to drink, almost as if I'd jinx my progress if I said it too loudly. "I came up with a great idea today." I removed one of the chess pieces from my pocket and handed it to him. "It may not look like much, but it's got an important role to play in getting you better."

Before Finley could finish his smoothie, we were interrupted by a knock at the door. I forced Finley to hold the shaker and snatched the queen out of his hand, stuffing it back in my pocket. I rushed over to the door and opened it a crack to peer into the hallway. Devon's piercing blue eyes peered back at me, his lips rising to a smile. He now had a key to my room due to Finley, but he knew not to abuse it—to knock unless I'd previously asked him to check on my brother.

"You survived," Devon said. He glanced around the hallway, then added, "The coast is clear."

"I'm pretty tired," I said while opening the door to let him in. "It was a lot of work. We cleaned windows. Picked up trash. Shoveled snow."

"There are ways to make all that stuff easier."

"No magic," I said, feeling like a broken record. "It was like the whole point of the punishment. Not like it was anything new to me. I'd been doing stuff like that my whole life. But a full day of it is still a lot of work. My back and shoulders are killing me."

"I'm sure I can help with that too," he said, placing a kiss on my cheek and sitting on my bed. "Hey, Finley."

I took the empty shaker from Finley, who barely acknowledged that Devon was even here, then he lay back down on the bed, turning to face the wall.

"Come here," Devon instructed. When I did, he sat me between his legs, then went to work at digging the knots out of my back and shoulders.

"Oh, God... that feels *so* good," I breathed, not realizing how sexual it sounded until the words had escaped my lips. I cringed at the thought of Finley hearing it—though he was probably tuning me out completely. Still, I made sure to keep my mouth shut as Devon continued to melt all the soreness and tension from my body.

And after another ten minutes, I couldn't even sit up under my own power anymore. I leaned back into him and he wrapped his strong arms around me. His breath warmed my neck, which then tingled as he trailed quiet kisses along my skin.

"Thank you," I finally said. "I needed that." My body leaned to the side, and Devon repositioned himself to allow me to lie down. I stretched an arm under my pillow and got myself comfortable. "I'm so tired."

"I thought, maybe, you'd want to go out," Devon said. "After all, it *is* Saturday night. Maybe, you'd want to come over to my room?"

"I'd like that," I said, gazing up at his hopeful face. "But not tonight. I really am tired as all hell."

Devon's expression sank, looking like I'd stomped all over his hopes and dreams. However, he didn't try to convince me further.

"I understand," he said as he rose from the bed.

Even though I wasn't ready for bed, he shimmied the blankets down around my body until they were freed to tuck me in. He finished with kissing me on the forehead, then left the room.

A great part of me wanted to spend the night with him, but I really was exhausted—it hadn't been a line—and there was a small sense of satisfaction at turning him down like he'd done to me on the first night here. It may have been petty, but it helped me feel more in control. And there wasn't much I felt in control of these days, which terrified me.

CHAPTER 23

I passed by Alexi in between classes on Monday and we shared a look that said *don't screw with me*. I'd probably passed by her numerous times before and never noticed. I had a feeling I'd now be seeing her everywhere. Maybe that was a good thing—a constant reminder that she and her friends couldn't truly hurt me. However, I was still skeptical of that protection spell she said had been placed on me to ensure I didn't freeze to death.

With that thought, I wanted to know more about the protective spell Professor Windsor had given me, which I hadn't inquired too deeply about after receiving it. And I planned to do just that after Combative Casting. I first had to get through the class, which was always a challenge.

Instead of throwing each other out of the circle,

today we started working on moving each other out of it. It was a similar exercise to what I'd been practicing with Devon, except desks didn't actively fight to remain in place. This exercise had that extra layer of complexity.

Nym and I sat within the circle—*crisscross applesauce*—and I tried to push her backward in my mind while splitting my focus to keep her from moving me. It was an invisible war. And kind of like watching paint dry.

I couldn't even feel anything for about half the class, and I didn't know if I was getting anywhere with Nym. So, I just had to ask her, unable to take the monotony anymore.

"Nym, do you feel anything?" I asked.

"No... I'm assuming you don't either. We probably should be—"

"No talking," Professor Windsor snapped as she passed behind me. "If you're talking, then you're not fully focused on the task at hand. You need all your energy and focus if you want any hoped-for results."

"Sorry," I said, not even turning to look at her. I remained focused on the tricky elf before me.

"You're still talking." She was walking away, but I was sure the comment was still aimed at us.

I did what I could to clear my mind—to block out everything else in my life so I could be entirely present for this exercise. Well, that was easier said than done because there was always a lot of shit going on in my life. Today was no exception.

More thoughts crept into my head of how I was going to get the dagger and if my plan to replace the chess piece was going to work, and what I was going to find in Kicryria when I finally made it there. At least there was no doubt there—one way or another, I was going to make it.

But as more of these thoughts took over, it became harder and harder to quiet my mind and return to the singular focus the exercise required. Maybe if I'd still had my needle or crystal, I'd be able to still get some results with these distractions. Without my amplifiers, everything was ten times freakin' harder. I was putting in a lot of extra hours of practice, but still hadn't made up for the deficit.

I shifted in my seated position, my glutes beginning to cramp. Wait… My glutes were starting to cramp because I was flexing, ensuring I stayed in place. I hadn't intentionally shifted. It wasn't a voluntary movement. I was pushed by some unseen force.

Nym, you tricky little elf.

I stared her down, the other thoughts that had crept in vanishing instantaneously. There was nothing like a push to challenge me to push back— and I always pushed back harder.

Nym had a smile on her face now. She knew what she'd done, but wasn't about to break her concentration by sharing. She was simply doubling her efforts, and I had to do the same.

"You can't move an immovable object," I said quietly. Professor Windsor was halfway across the room and wouldn't have been able to hear me, but Nym with her superhuman hearing most certainly could. I'd break my concentration just long enough to break hers. I needed to get in her head. "I am rooted to the ground like the mighty oak."

I knew it sounded cheesy, but it was working. She knew that *I knew*, and that realization would start messing with her confidence and concentration. I needed to take any advantage where I could find one.

I pushed Nym in my mind over and over, yet she didn't move from her spot. I didn't even know if my magical assaults were actually reaching her or registering at all on her radar. So far, she wasn't letting on like they were. But as I began to focus more on her reactions than my own actions, I realized I was headed in the wrong direction.

I felt another nudge, then a push—then a full-on tidal wave forcing me back a few inches. All my attention went to defense as the invisible water kept flowing toward me until I was fully caught in the current. Before I could stop it, I was skidding backward and crossing the white line on the floor.

"I win!" Nym exclaimed, throwing up her hands in victory.

As soon as she reveled in her victory, the current steadily drained until the opposing force was gone. I dropped onto my back, breathing heavily from the strain of fighting to remain in position.

"You won this round, little elf," I said between labored breaths. "But don't get too cocky. The war is far from over."

"Nice work, Nym," Professor Windsor said, standing over me. "Now you know what it feels like and will be better prepared for the next time."

I didn't know if that second part was directed at Nym or me, but I had a feeling it applied to both of us.

After a two-minute rest, I was back in the circle and ready to go again. The remainder of the class was a stalemate. I wasn't sure I moved her an inch, but I didn't get caught up in her current again. I felt it as it was coming and was able to better defend myself.

Instead of getting frustrated for not securing another victory, Nym was proud of me for holding her off.

Only Nym.

When class ended, I told Nym I'd catch up with her and Razielle in a few minutes, then waited for the students to file out of the classroom.

"I know it's hard not having your needle," Professor Windsor said. "And to top it off, your crystal was taken away. I understand how frustrating that is. But sometimes, losses are more important than victories. They teach you better strategies for next time. They reveal where you're weakest, so you can work on correcting that chink in your armor. They can provide powerful lessons. You did well today."

"Thank you," I said. "But that's not why I'm here."

"Oh?"

"I wanted to ask you about the protective spell you put on me a few weeks ago. What exactly is it doing? I was so concerned before with what the Kicryrians could possibly be using my blood for that I didn't even think to ask."

"And what's gotten you to ask now?" she asked.

"I just thought about it over the weekend—realized I'd never asked—kind of like taking medicine and forgetting to read up on the side effects."

"Well, for one, there are no side effects," Professor Windsor said with an unsuspecting laugh. "The spell I placed on you protects you from quite a few things. Most importantly, your body cannot be manipulated. So, your fears can be eased about the Kicryrians controlling you remotely. That won't be possible. But the spell also keeps you safe from the elements. You'll be affected by them, but they won't kill you. Fire. Frostbite. Water—or drowning. Air—you won't suffocate. Even electricity. Even though these things won't be able to kill you, you might wish they would. Your brain will still react to the pain such assaults would warrant. You just wouldn't be given the reprieve of death."

"That sounds terrible," I said. "Why would you—"

"The point is not for you jump into a fire because you can," the professor explained. "The point is to be able to survive the worst if the worst were to arise. So, don't go getting any crazy ideas of your invincibility."

"Will the spell stop a bullet?"

Professor Windsor stared at me incredulously, obviously wondering why I'd ask such a question. "The spell does not make you impenetrable. And remember, it doesn't numb the pain. It also doesn't stop you from bleeding out. That would require a healing spell in the moment. I'd seriously advise against jumping in the middle of gunfights."

"Duly noted," I said.

When I left the Manor, I looked around the grounds for Nym and Razielle, but they weren't hanging around in the winter cold. At least it wasn't snowing today. Given Razielle's track record, they were probably in the cafeteria getting a mid-afternoon snack. For Razielle, that meant more like second lunch.

Instead of returning to the cafeteria, I decided to head back to my room and check on Finley since I hadn't stopped in at lunchtime. But when I arrived, I was greeted with another unwanted visitor.

"You're back," I said, instantly reverting to my

death glare at the sight of Guy. "What the hell are you doing here?"

"Hey, Maeve," he said like this was just another casual visit.

"Don't *hey Maeve* me," I shot back. "You can't just show up here whenever you feel like it. I didn't turn you in last time since you brought back my brother, but I'm not going to keep allowing this."

"I was just dropping off a little gift for Fin."

Fin. I not only cringed—the name literally made my eye twitch.

"And I wanted to make sure he was still doing okay, considering his condition." Guy glanced at my brother, then back at me. "He's not looking good. He needs to eat more."

"No shit, Sherlock," I said. "Tell *him* that. I have to continually force feed him."

"I'm doing what I can to get him help, but for now, this is still the safest place for him."

"What does that mean?"

"I can't help him if you turn me in, so please keep that in mind." Guy advanced toward the door, but I blocked his path.

"Who has my needle?"

"You don't want to know."

"I *need* to know," I insisted. "You want to keep me from turning you in, then throw me a freakin' bone."

"Tarquin Drome," Guy said. "The friendly and approachable guy you met in the tower."

"That's not funny," I said. I recognized the name and remembered the face—and the first time I'd seen lips sewn shut with red thread. And that horrible voice that sounded directly into my brain like a nightmare. "He killed Devon's father. He killed Helena."

"He's killed lots of people. He wasn't supposed to steal the needle like he did, but none of us could stop him."

"Yeah; he didn't seem like the listening type."

"He's an Elite Forces lieutenant, like your father used to be." Guy stopped, allowing me to absorb what he'd just said,

"My father?" I asked. Headmistress Christi had mentioned about my father being a lieutenant in the Kicryrian army—but Elite Forces? I'd never thought of my father as an Elite Forces kind of guy.

"I obviously didn't know him, but I'd heard of him," Guy said. "He was a well-respected leader and fighter—at least by most people. Everyone who excels and rises in the ranks makes enemies."

Finley was just watching us, listening intently to our conversation. I couldn't tell if this was news to him or not. I noticed something cupped in his hand, then saw the end of a chain dangling over the side of his palm.

"What's that?" I asked. I pushed past Guy to get a better look at what seemed to be a soul crystal.

Finley opened his hand to reveal I was right. I was ecstatic.

"Is that what I think it is?" I asked, turning back to Guy—but he was already gone, the door still in mid swing.

CHAPTER 24

*T*raced into the hallway, and when I didn't immediately see Guy, I continued through the lobby and out into the cold afternoon air. I advanced onto the sidewalk to get out of Windsor Hall's shadow, then searched the grounds in all directions.

Guy was gone—again. That slippery son of a bitch.

Tired of chasing after a ghost, I headed back inside. Finley was still sitting up on his bed, palm open, clearly displaying the soul crystal.

"Is that the gift he brought?" I asked.

Finley nodded and offered me the crystal.

In my hands, it didn't start to glow, but I could feel its power—its energy—as a warmth washed over me. "Is it Mom?"

Again, Finley nodded.

I felt tears prickle the edges of my eyes at the mere thought of having her back. My hands were literally shaking. It was like she was alive again. If only she were here to hug me. So, I did the next best thing. I dropped to the bed beside Finley and wrapped my arms around him and cried. There was no way I could hold back the tears. And for once, I wasn't ashamed.

When I finally let go of my brother, I realized he was crying as well. The floodgates had opened for both of us, and all we could do was go with it.

When I went to place the crystal back in his hand, Finley wouldn't take it. He pushed my hand away before drying his eyes.

"Thank you," I said, mirroring the action and drying my own eyes. I slipped on the necklace and immediately felt my mother's love and warmth. I wanted to know so much about her, but guessed I'd have to settle for her silent embrace. I knew I wouldn't be able to get away with wearing it outside, but in the safety of my own room, I wanted her close to my heart.

I walked over to my desk and retrieved a pencil. Leaning against the desk, I touched the tip of the pencil to my forefinger, balanced it, then let go. I remembered the difficulty I'd had with balancing a pencil back at the apartment and numerous times afterward. With some focused effort, I'd been able to do it. This time, I was still focused, but the pencil balanced with no effort at all. I didn't have to move my hand around to keep it balanced. The pencil was balancing on its own—obeying my mental command like it had no other choice.

Slowly, I began to move my hand, not in an attempt to keep it balanced, but to see if the pencil would continue to obey and move in perfect unison with my hand. It did and remained perfectly upright.

Finley was intently watching me, and his sewn lips curled up into a smile as I dropped my hand while the pencil remained suspended in midair. That had been what Finley did when he'd first met Otis and I'd given him the first prick of the needle. That seemed like a lifetime ago.

"I'm hopeful for the first time in a while," I said, snatching the pencil out of the air. "Thanks, Mom. With you, I feel like I can do anything."

Between my reunion with my mother's crystal and what I'd learned about the protection spell, I truly felt invincible.

CHAPTER 25

"Scoot over," I told Nym as I came to sit beside her on the cafeteria bench. However, before she had the chance to oblige, her body and tray slid a foot to the left. The fact that she wasn't touching her tray made the action even more impressive.

To say the least, Nym was shocked. Ivanic and Bree were sitting across from her, and their eyes went wide as well.

"*Damn*," Ivanic said, laughing. "Maeve is back with the tricks."

"Yes, I am," I said with a knowing grin as I took a seat beside Nym. She wasn't giving me the look she had when I'd thrown her from the circle on the first day of school, but it was close. The crystal was warm in my pocket, my secret weapon.

"I love you." He batted his eyes at me.

"Don't get any freakin' ideas," I warned. "You know what I'm willing to do. And I don't think you want to be walking back to Windsor Hall in your boxers in the snow."

"I could just shift," he reminded me. "I rarely get cold as a cougar."

"All I heard was boxers, snow, and cougars," Razielle said, coming around the table and taking a seat next to Ivanic. "Fill me in."

"You have very selective hearing," I said.

"Yeah, I listen for the juicy bits." She was giving Ivanic no room, but he didn't seem to mind—or notice. "So really, what is it—a dare or something?"

"No, just a punishment if cougar boy doesn't lay off the Romeo act," I said.

"Leave the poor girl alone!" Razielle exclaimed, backhanding Ivanic in the arm. "She's spoken for. There are plenty of girls around here who aren't."

I suspected she was talking about herself, but however brazen she could be with comments and innuendos, she didn't seem capable of seriously asking him out.

"What can I say? She's got my heart," Ivanic said, then took a sip of his milk as if to taunt me. "Oh, crap. I guess it's time to behave."

I turned my head to where Ivanic was looking and saw Devon approaching our table with a full tray of food. He joined us more regularly for dinners, not lunches, so this was a nice surprise.

"Hey, guys," he said as he took a seat beside me, then kissed me on the cheek. "Hey, you."

He was in better spirits after being denied Saturday night. Perhaps we were on an even playing field again. Neither of us could take what we had for granted.

Unfortunately, when Devon arrived, the energy in the group changed and there wasn't a damn thing I could do about it. He wasn't really part of the group and he never would be.

The conversation for the rest of lunch remained light and Ivanic behaved himself. Erik and Sarah didn't show up until the rest of us were about ready to leave.

"You missed a button," I said to Erik, who immediately glanced down at his shirt.

"That's embarrassing," he said, but his tone and pallor didn't suggest that he actually was embarrassed. However, Sarah's cheeks flushed a little and she dug straight into her food to distract herself.

After lunch, Devon pulled me aside upon exiting the cafeteria, taking my gloved hand in his. "Can we talk?" he asked.

"Of course, but it's about time for class to start," I said, not liking the sound of his voice. "What's up?"

"I just want to make sure we're okay," he said. "*Are* we okay? I mean, I know things have been hard since last year and we still had our issues at the beginning of this year. But are we good now?"

"Yeah," I said, casually. "I'm not torturing you out of a grudge, if that's what you mean. I'm not like that. I'll tell you what's up, and that's that."

"I didn't think you were," Devon said and slid a gloved hand down my cold cheek. "But I just wanted to make sure we were... umm—good. I know you have to look after your brother now and that's stressful too."

"It has its challenges, that's for sure," I said, thinking of all the nights we set the alarm in the middle of the night, so he could safely use the first-floor boys' bathroom to shower, wash up, and do whatever else he'd been holding in.

"If there was more on your mind—more you needed help with or something—you'd tell me, right?"

I sure as hell hoped he didn't have some power of reading minds. His question was eerie. "I'm just trying to catch up with my school work and severely hindered abilities. You know, all the normal stuff us neophytes have to deal with on a daily basis."

"Your abilities are returning," he said. "I've seen it in practice."

I smiled, knowing he hadn't seen anything yet. "That's true. I *am* starting to kick ass again."

"Maeve, we've gotta go," Nym said from farther down the sidewalk, where only she and Razielle were left.

Devon planted his icy lips on mine. "Go kick some more ass in Combative Casting," he said.

"Oh, I intend to," I said with a laugh—nearly snorting.

That little elf isn't gonna know what hit her.

I rejoined Nym and Razielle, heading back to the Manor. It was just starting to snow again. The wind was whipping across my face. And I didn't feel cold at all. I felt absolutely wonderful.

"Are you ready for this, little elf?" I asked, a big smile plastered across my face.

Nym looked about the opposite of ready, her pointy ears twitching. I assumed that was a nervous twitch. I'd never asked.

"Why are you so happy?" Razielle asked. "Did you get some and not tell me about it?"

"Not that at all," I said. "Better."

"Better than sex?"

"Power is so much better than sex."

"Maybe you're not doing it right."

I wrapped a leather arm around the unabashed Nephilim and squeezed. "I *know* I'm doing it right. And as incredible as it is, it isn't the best thing in the world. Now, we need to talk after class. I've got some ideas. No more stalling. It's time to get that fucking dagger."

CHAPTER 26

*N*ym had no idea what hit her. And now Professor Windsor was back to thinking I'd been holding back. No one suspected I had a crystal again. Having my mother literally in my pocket seemed to give me so much more power than the crystal I'd lost to the headmistress. I almost felt like I had my needle again, even though I knew the change couldn't be that drastic.

After class, we made plans to meet up late. My alarm was set for the normal 2 a.m. wakeup call, so Finley could safely freshen up in the bathroom. But instead of going back to sleep, I got dressed and met the girls outside. The clouds had cleared, leaving behind a moonless star-filled sky.

"Got the dagger?" I asked Razielle.

"Yup. You got the queen?" she asked in return.

She lifted one side of her coat to reveal the paper-wrapped dagger, secured with packing tape.

"I wouldn't leave home without it," I said, patting the front pocket of my black jeans. Then I turned to Nym. She wasn't looking so good. "You're not gonna pass out on us, are you?"

She shook her head, but it still wasn't convincing.

"Now's the time," I said. "You can go back to bed right now. You don't have to do this."

"I'm coming," she said, sounding slightly more convincing.

That was all I needed to hear. We headed over to the Manor, Razielle leading us back to Professor Voltaire's office because I would have gotten us lost. We hadn't seen a single person since leaving Windsor Hall, which was a good start.

Standing outside the door, I placed my hand on the knob and envisioned the thumb-turn lock on the backside of the door. I could feel it between my fingers, turning smoothly and easily. As I glanced in through the glass in the door, I saw the lock turning on its own, followed by a click. I turned the knob and the door opened.

"You did it!" Razielle whisper-yelled.

But before I could revel in my accomplishment, Nym spoke up. "Someone's coming."

I hadn't heard anything, but that was why we had her—to help us hear what we couldn't.

The three of us dashed inside the dark office, the

girls skirting to the side, and me ducking under the line of glass and carefully closing the door from my knees. The click of the bolt sliding into place sounded awfully loud.

As I turned the lock, the beam of a flashlight shone into the office through the glass in the door, methodically moving around the room. Then the door knob jiggled as whoever was outside tried to turn it.

I thought my pounding heart might give us away as it thrummed erratically in my chest. Razielle was flat against the wall and Nym was crouched behind a chair. No one moved.

The flashlight beam did one more sweep of the room, then vanished. I listened carefully to the sound of footsteps walking away from the door, then let out a long breath.

"The person's gone," Nym said, and I knew she was a better judge of how far away the footsteps were. I trusted Nym's enhanced elven abilities.

"How about anyone else?" I asked before moving from my spot against the door.

"I don't hear anyone else," she said.

"That's good enough for me," Razielle said, pushing off from her spot against the wall.

I followed her lead, stood, and ventured into the room. Razielle removed the wrapped dagger from under her shirt and began to peel off the tape.

Nym walked straight over to the dagger on the

wall inside the glass case, then looked around as if she was searching for which piece of furniture would be best to climb on to reach the frame.

We hadn't specifically discussed that detail, but I'd thought it was obvious. So did Razielle, because as soon as she was done unwrapping the dagger, she placed it on the desk and removed her coat. The shirt she was wearing underneath had long vertical slits in the back. She stretched and straightened her shoulders before her elegant ivory wings burst from her back. She was standing too close to the desk when she did and knocked over a few picture frames positioned near the corner. The distinct sound of breaking glass filled the room.

"Shit," Razielle muttered under her breath, immediately picking up the fallen frames. The one that had a smiling picture of a young girl I could only assume was his daughter was cracked in numerous places. "No turning back now."

Then all the lights in the room suddenly came on. The three of us spun around, expecting to see someone standing in the doorway, even though Nym hadn't heard anyone. But there was no one there. The door was still closed. No one was looking through the glass. For all the world, we seemed to still be alone.

But the room was now extremely bright—squint-worthy bright. The few animal heads on the walls came to life, eyes finding and following us as we moved around the room. A stone sculpture of a muscular man in a toga was set on a small table in one corner of the room. It stood about three feet tall, and the man's head was also moving, his eyes blinking, as his attention was also trained on us.

"What the hell's going on?" Razielle cried.

Nym froze, petrified of all these unnatural eyes on her.

"Hurry up!" I said. "This is our one shot!"

Razielle quickly took flight and retrieved the glass case from high up on the wall. She placed it on the ground and examined the back of the case, trying to figure out how to open it. Then a frustrated sigh escaped her lips. "It requires a screwdriver."

"Let me see it," I said, crouching beside her while Nym continued to look on from above. It was true, the backing was held on by eight screws. But then I thought for a second. This was no different than moving a desk, a pencil, a Nym. I just needed the screws to move in a counter-clockwise direction.

I focused on the screw in the upper righthand corner, pulling it toward me. The crystal in my pocket felt warm, and I knew in some strange way my mother was helping me.

"Holy crap! You're doing it!" Razielle exclaimed.

But I had to block her out, otherwise my concentration would be compromised. Then I remembered the exercise Professor Windsor had us do in the snow. The non-ideal conditions were important to master because they required you to truly master your mind.

Well, the lights blaring and dead animals watching us work was pretty freakin' non-ideal. So, I kept going, and soon the first screw fell out of the frame.

Seven more to go.

"I hear something," Nym said. "It's faint, but there's someone else around. I can't tell yet if they're coming in our direction."

"Go faster," Razielle said.

"I'm going as fast as I can," I argued, not taking my attention away from the next screw I was working on. This one was coming out faster than the first. And by the time I got to the third screw, two of them were inching out of the frame at the same time.

I put every ounce of energy and concentration into the last four screws and miraculously got them all moving counter-clockwise simultaneously. As soon as they were all out, I dug my nails into the edges of the frame and removed the backing. That was when I noticed something was terribly wrong…

"What the hell?" I cried out.

The girls joined me in looking into the glass case, quickly discovering it was empty.

"Where did it go?" Nym asked.

"How the hell should I know?" I snapped, probably more harshly than I'd intended. But this was a *big* problem. The whole reason we were here was because of the dagger in this case—the dagger that *had been* in this case.

"The footsteps are definitely coming closer," Nym said. She was back to glancing around the room to find a place to hide. "My parents are gonna kill me."

"No one's gonna kill you," I said.

Nym ran for the door, then supplied us with more bad news. "It's locked!"

"Then unlock it," Razielle said.

"I know how to unlock a door. I think it's magically locked."

"Then *magically* unlock it."

"We need to hide." Nym was frantically searching the room—the animal heads still following her every move.

I didn't know what to do about the dagger, but we were out of time. I joined Nym in the search for somewhere to hide, then looked up and noticed the tiles in the ceiling.

"Razielle, can you get us up there?" I asked.

She followed my gaze. "I—I dunno. You guys are heavy."

"Nym can't be that heavy. She's thin as a rail," I said. "Just try."

Razielle flew to the high ceiling and lifted one of the square tiles, pushing it into the ceiling. "There's space," she said from above us.

"Then get us up there," I said. "Nym first."

Razielle returned to the ground, hooked her arms under Nym's armpits, and attempted to lift the two of them off the ground. Her wings flapped furiously, the wind storm they created knocking over more small items. Razielle was off the ground, but she was still tugging and straining to lift Nym.

"You can do it," I said, trying to remain calm and encouraging. I would have thought she'd have done this before with friends. She certainly never looked weak to me.

As soon as Nym's feet were airborne, Razielle seemed to get her confidence and the two of them shot up to the ceiling in a flash. First, Razielle helped Nym climb into the space above the ceiling. Then she was ready to drop to the floor for me.

"Stop!" I urged just as I saw the beam of a flashlight at the door. "Just go! Get out of here!"

Razielle turned her attention toward the door, her face going white as she realized what was happening. She gave me an empathetic look before following Nym into the ceiling, replacing the tile just as the door burst open.

CHAPTER 27

"What's going on in here?" a demanding angry voice asked. A large man with a club of a flashlight and a bright blue crystal stood in the doorway, taking up nearly the entire open space.

I sprang to my feet, knowing it wouldn't do any good to hide. Even the toga-man statue was pointing in my direction. I had no excuse for being here, so I could say nothing or lie my ass off.

"I was going to decorate Professor Voltaire's office for his birthday, so he'd be like super surprised in the morning, when the room came to life and scared the shit out of me. I knocked over a bunch of stuff," I said, allowing all the fear I was feeling to come through in my voice.

"Who's in here with you?" The man stepped into

the room, turning off his flashlight since the room was so bright, and surveyed the damage.

"No one. I swear," I said. "This was all my bone-head idea. I didn't mean to mess anything up."

"Where are your decorations?" he asked, skeptically, now approaching me.

"Magical decorations," I said. "I didn't bring any." I pinched the tip of my right forefinger like I'd done previously to call forth my needle and pulled a red ribbon from my finger... which kept coming and coming until it was piling up at my feet. Then I seemed to reach the end of the ribbon, and I let it fall to the floor. "See?" I said, smugly. But inside, I was freaking out.

Holy shit! How did I just do that?

"I didn't know his birthday was coming up," the hulking man said. "But that still doesn't excuse a break in."

"Can I at least clean up?" I asked.

"I don't want you to touch anything else. It's all evidence."

"Evidence?"

"Let's go, kid." The man grabbed my upper arm, his fingers actually able to touch as they encircled my entire arm, and hauled me toward the door.

I didn't try to grab for anything because there was nothing else I needed. Our duplicate dagger didn't matter. The real dagger was gone, and I had no idea what we were going to do now. My entire plan had been relying on that damn dagger. I didn't know if the disappearing act was a protection spell or a decoy. Either way, I was back to square one.

"Can I go back to my room? It's pretty late. I can explain everything to Professor Voltaire tomorrow." I asked as he continued to walk me down the hallway.

"Not tonight," the man said, then added, "Give me your phone."

"Why?" I demanded, but instead of answering, he asked again—though *ask* wasn't really the right word.

"Either you give it to me or I take it from you. You've lost phone privileges for the evening."

"You make it sound like I'm in junior high," I said, though I handed it over instead of pressing my luck. I was already seemingly in enough trouble, and God only knew how much. "Where are we going?"

"Holding," was all he said, and still we walked.

The big man led me down two flights of stairs to the first floor, then headed deeper into the Manor. After a few more turns, we went through another doorway, which had another set of stairs leading down. The descending path ahead was pitch black, so he turned on his flashlight and led me into the abyss.

Are we going to the Crystal Crypt?

I figured asking any more questions would be

useless, so I kept my mouth shut and my eyes wide open.

The stone walls were familiar, but the space wasn't cavernous like the other times I was down here. We walked down a narrow stone hallway. At first, the walls were solid stone, but after we turned a corner, there were heavy metal doors built into the stone, reminiscent of a medieval dungeon.

After passing several closed doors, my guide stopped before one that was ajar. He pushed it open and instructed me to go inside.

"And if I don't?" I asked, defiantly. "This doesn't exactly seem legal—"

But as I was still talking, he pushed me, and I stumbled into the small room. Before I could recover, the door slammed shut behind me.

With the door closed, the room was shrouded in total darkness. For the split second before I'd lost the ability to see, I'd gotten a glimpse of a cot against one stone wall and a toilet built into another. I felt around the floor with my hands until I found the bed, climbed up, and sat on a mattress that wasn't much more forgiving than the stone floor.

Well, this sucks.

I retrieved the crystal from my pocket, hoping it would start glowing again and give me some light. But it didn't. In fact, it hadn't glowed since I'd gotten it back. I felt its warmth, but not a single ounce of light was exuded from the gem. So, I simply held it in my hand for comfort.

"Now what am I supposed to do?" I asked my mother, whose soul was trapped in here with me. I'd really felt like things would work out tonight, that I'd be closer to reaching Kicryria and getting my needle back. I knew it had always been a long shot, but with my mother returned to me, I felt I was holding the winning lottery ticket. But now, locked in this dungeon cell, it seemed like that winning vision was slipping away into the darkness.

I stood and placed my hands out in front of my body, slowly making my way to the door by memory. When my hands found the wall, I moved to one side until I found the corner of the room, then traced the wall in the opposite direction. Nothing. The wall seemed to be solid from one end to the other.

I circled the entire room, wondering if I'd just gotten disoriented and turned around in the dark. But the toilet and bed were exactly where I pictured them in my head. My fingers never found a break in the wall. The door was gone.

I was locked in a room with no exit, with no clue of what was coming next—if this was my holding cell while I awaited punishment, or if this *was* my punishment.

As the time dragged on, my imagination ran wild

with terrible things. At least Devon knew about Finley, so he wasn't left completely alone.

Please let Razielle and Nym out of this debacle unscathed. I hoped they were able to get out of the Manor and back to their room without getting caught.

As I continued to sit in utter darkness, trying to block the worst from consuming my thoughts, I transitioned to focusing on my training. Gripping the crystal tight and feeling the warmth flowing from the necklace into my hands, I managed to conjure a fiery ball of energy. Instead of shooting it at a target, I had it hover in the middle of the room to give me light.

Now I could confirm that where the door had been when I'd entered the room was indeed gone. I was inside a complete stone cube—no entrances or exits anywhere.

Stupid magic!

I instructed the flaming ball to crash into the wall where the door had been. Upon impact, the ball burst into a million orange sparks that rained to the ground and went out. I was back in the dark again.

That didn't work. Stupid magic.

Finally, I lay down onto the lumpy mattress and closed my eyes, which didn't change the level of darkness whatsoever. I could conjure another energy ball, but what was the point? Instead, I decided to save my energy. I didn't know what I'd need it for, but I didn't want to be on empty.

I slipped in and out of a dreamlike state for what felt like hours, afraid of what I'd wake up to if I did fall asleep.

When a light appeared in the room, I didn't know if I was still dreaming. It took me a few moments of rubbing my eyes to realize the door had been opened and a man I'd never seen before was standing in the doorway. A lantern with green fire flickering inside the protective glass hung from one hand. He was probably half the size of the guy from last night, but he looked every bit as intense, giving a hard stare, his lips nothing more than a flat line across his face.

"Get up," the man demanded, his voice sounding almost like a growl. His arms were covered in so much hair, it almost looked like fur.

My back was killing me as I rose from the sadistic cot. I was still holding the crystal and quickly stuffed it in my pocket.

"Am I free to go?" I asked as I made my way out of the cell.

"Not quite," the man said with an unnerving chuckle. Instead of elaborating, he simply walked away, intending for me to follow.

Since absolute blackness swallowed the hallway in the opposite direction, I saw no choice but to follow. And it probably wouldn't have been smart to get myself into more trouble since I still didn't know what awaited me.

I was led back up the stairs to the main floor of the Manor, where there were already students roaming the halls, though not many. It was either still early in the morning or classes had already started. As we walked by the main entrance, I saw it was light outside.

Then the doors opened and Nym strolled into the foyer. We locked eyes but didn't say anything. I was so thankful she'd made it out, but I couldn't stop to wonder where Razielle was. I wanted to stop and ask her, but didn't want to drag her further into this mess, so I smiled and kept right on walking. Nym returned my smile, but hers was noticeably pained— an expression that made me more nervous.

The hairy man turned to now lead me upstairs, and I wondered if we were heading back to Professor Voltaire's office. But when we didn't stop at the third floor, I had a pretty good idea where he was taking me.

We proceeded all the way to the fifth floor and down the hallway, stopping before the invisible door 504 ¾. He ran his hand along the wall until he found the door, opened it into the physical world, and ordered me inside.

"The headmistress is expecting you," he said, a wicked grin spreading over his lips, revealing sharp teeth.

CHAPTER 28

*J*anuary snow was falling all around the headmistress's office. She was seated on the far couch, staring intently at her phone, her reading glasses far down on her nose.

I dragged my feet as I approached the couches, though she didn't look up until I'd reached the sitting space.

"Please, have a seat, Maeve," she said, setting the phone on the cushion beside her and removing her reading glasses. They were on a chain and hung at her neck over her crystal.

As I did, I glanced at the phone, realizing it wasn't hers—but mine. My mind immediately went to all the text messages I'd had with Devon, having no idea how she'd taken them.

I guess I'm about to find out.

"Would you like to start by explaining what you

were doing in Professor Voltaire's office last night? And I don't want to hear the stupid excuse of decorating the room for his birthday. His birthday's in June."

"Wouldn't that make it more surprising?" I asked with a delirious laugh. I hadn't gotten much sleep and was running on fumes.

Headmistress Christi glared at me, clearly not amused.

What was I supposed to tell her? We were trying to steal the Seam Dagger? I really should have come up with a backup story beforehand, for just such an occasion. But in the end, the best lies were based in truth.

"I needed to get my hands on the Seam Dagger," I said, getting right to the point.

"How do you know about it and what would you plan to do with it?" she asked, crossing her legs as well as her arms as she impatiently awaited my response. Though as angry and skeptical as she seemed, she stayed on her couch. She didn't come over to my couch to give me the *touch of truth*.

"To find my brother," I said. "I know he was taken to Kicryria. I need to get him back. He's everything to me."

"The same brother who stole your needle?" Her tone was mocking.

"I don't believe he did it under his own free will. I believe he was coerced."

"And what makes you believe that?"

"Because he's my brother. I've known him my whole life and *know* he'd never really do that to me."

"Power and the possibility of power can do strange and dangerous things. It can turn ally against ally, friend against friend... brother against sister."

"He wouldn't do that to me," I said, glaring back at her with the conviction that I actually believed it. Surprisingly, a part of me still did. It wasn't like I could actually ask him about it yet.

"Be that as it may, you must at least consider the possibility," the headmistress said. "Now, how did you learn about the Seam Dagger?"

I had to think for a minute because I didn't want to drag Razielle into this. "The guy that my brother started hanging out with last trimester—Guy, coincidentally—he was a Master Classman and before everything went down, he'd mentioned it at one point. I couldn't remember the professor's name, so I had to do a little research of my own."

"I see." The headmistress was working through something in her mind. "And here we are. You performed this intended act of thievery alone?"

I nodded, confidently.

"You've had a very difficult start to the trimester. And I've already warned you to stay out of trouble. One of your motivators was to get your crystal back, but that didn't provide as much motivation as I was hoping it would. Perhaps, that's because you didn't need a replacement after all." She paused to judge my reaction.

I did my best to remain straight-faced, trying not to give anything away, but somehow it seemed I already had.

"Give me the new crystal you acquired," she demanded and held out a hand.

"I don't have a—"

"Give it to me!"

"Please…" I pleaded. "Please just let me keep it. I won't do anything else outside of my schoolwork. I'll do everything else you ask. Please…" If I told her why the crystal was so important, then she'd want to know how I'd gotten it back. And even if I didn't, she'd be able to see whose soul was trapped inside and come back to me with the same question. I didn't see how I could get myself out of this one.

"I won't ask you again." Her voice was quieter now, but twice as menacing.

I had no idea how she knew about the new crystal, though I had little choice but to comply. I pulled the soul crystal from my pocket and placed it in her outstretched hand.

She examined it, then picked it up by the chain and allowed it to dangle in front of her, watching as it swung back and forth like a pendulum. Her expression turned to that of confusion as she grabbed onto the edge of the crystal and held it out. Maybe she was wondering why the crystal still wasn't glowing, a question that had plagued me since getting it back.

"Did you realize you were carrying around an empty crystal?" she finally asked.

Empty? WTF?

"I'll deduce from that confounded expression, you didn't." Headmistress Christi set the crystal down on the cushion next to my phone. "It doesn't do much without the powers of a harnessed soul. But if you believed it was an active soul crystal, then no doubt you performed better with it. Placebos can sometimes be nearly as powerful as the real thing."

I couldn't believe that my mother wasn't in the crystal, which only meant she was still in Kicryria and Guy hadn't given her up after all.

That lying son of a bitch.

Or had Guy never said that. He'd told Finley something—some significance to the crystal. Had Finley been the one who'd lied with the nod of his head? I couldn't believe I'd let myself get duped again.

"If you were just about any other student, you'd be gone by now—your memory erased and dropped back into your old life. But with everything you've been through since you've been here, I'm inclined to give you one more chance. But I need you to forget about chasing after your brother and return your focus to the classroom. Those far more powerful than you are dealing with the latest threat. We *will* retrieve the lost needle. So, you should forget about it. It is no longer your concern. What *is* your concern is passing your classes and staying out of trouble.

"I know much more about what goes on here than you realize, and I won't continue to be deceived. Worry about your future. Worry about the futures of your friends. I don't want any of them going down a troublesome path because of your careless ideas and direction."

"I'll do better," I said. "I promise."

"I trust you will because I'm sure you don't want to ruin the future of any more of your trusting friends."

"What are you talking about?" I asked, sensing a threat.

"I know you weren't alone last night. The animals revealed who was in the room. You had two accomplices," the headmistress said, stopping for a moment to let that last line sink in.

Then I remembered seeing Nym without Razielle. "What did you do?"

"It's not what *I* did," she said. "It's what *you* forced me to do. Your friend, Razielle Valentine, is already on a flight home due to the stunt the three of you pulled last night. She's been expelled. I can do the same to Nym Uriro, but I'll wait to see how you cooperate. I believe the fate of your friends will be a bigger motivator than a direct threat against your status here. If that's not the case, then I can let the two of you go right now."

"Please don't do that," I begged. "Nym is a kind and wonderful person, as well as a model student— when she's not following me. Please don't make an example out of her because of my mistakes. If you need to send me home, then do it—but not her." As I pleaded for Nym's future at the Academy, I felt oncoming tears for the loss of Razielle. It was so hard to believe she was already gone—and all because of me. The sad smile I'd received from Nym this morning had to have been alluding to her already knowing the fate of her roommate.

"If you behave, then Nym will have nothing to worry about. But if you step out of line again, then you and Nym will never step foot in Spellcrest again. Do I make myself clear?"

"Crystal," I said.

The headmistress picked up my phone and offered it back to me. "You should get to class. You've missed enough as it is."

"Yes, ma'am," I said and walked over to her to take it. I didn't even want to know how many crazy messages I had by this point. Instead of rounding the opposite side of the coffee table, I proceeded past the headmistress, but my foot hooked hers and I went tumbling forward.

I tried to regain my balance, but stumbled a few more steps only to slam into the small table propping up the coveted chess board. Everything crashed to the floor, including me. The numerous chess pieces scattered like marbles.

Headmistress Christi was on her feet in a flash and rushed over, though I doubted much, if any, of her urgency had to do with my wellbeing.

"I'm *so* sorry," I cried, scrambling to my hands and knees and scooping up as many chess pieces as I could reach.

"Step away. Step away," she ordered, tugging at my coat to pull me to my feet.

Once I was standing, I gave her the handful of pieces I'd already gathered. She took them from me, then righted the table and set back the board. She poured the handful of pieces onto the board, then took a step back. With a wave of her hand, the pieces that were still on the floor flew onto the board and found their correct positions. Within seconds, the chess set was magically returned to how it looked before I slammed into it.

Almost.

"I'm sorry," I said again. "I tripped."

"Accidents happen," she said, taking none of the blame.

"It's a very nice set."

"It was a gift."

"I've always wanted to learn to play."

"It's a game of strategy and patience," she said,

then turned her attention to the snow falling outside. "Run along. We both have work to do."

I didn't need to be told twice. I rushed straight for the stairs in the center of the room and ran down them as fast as I could. Once I reached the fifth-floor hallway, I slowed and let out a long breath. I stuffed my left hand into my jeans front pocket and removed the new queen I'd managed to acquire at great risk and great personal satisfaction. And as I'd remembered, the bottom was labeled with a neatly-scrawled "Kicryria."

At least one good thing came out of this disaster.

With the queen in my possession, I had the means to get back from Kicryria. Now I just needed the means to get there. And I was sure the clock was ticking.

CHAPTER 29

"You lied to me about the crystal!" I yelled at my brother. Well, I wasn't really yelling because I didn't want anyone outside of our room to hear us—me. But I made sure the tone of my voice relayed how upset I was.

He vehemently shook his head like he hadn't just betrayed me again.

"Don't shake your head at me, little man. Mom wasn't in that soul crystal according to the head-mistress. No one was. It was an empty crystal—as in no soul in it. Did Guy tell you she was in there?"

Finley shook his head again.

"But you told me she was in there."

Finley nodded.

"Then why did you lie?"

He shook his head.

"Fuck; I'm so confused!" I said, exasperated. I went over to the desk and picked up the notebook I'd tried using with Finley when he'd first arrived. "Tell me what the hell you meant." I jabbed the notebook in his face.

Finley shook his head again.

"Yes!" I demanded.

Finley reluctantly took the notebook, then the pencil when I handed it to him. He flipped to a blank page, just past the page of scribbles he'd done last time. With a shaking hand, he brought the tip of the pencil to paper and slowly tried to control it as the first line formed. Then his arm just seemed to spasm out of control, connecting lines and curves all over the page. There were no words. Not even a clear picture. Then he was pressing so hard that the paper ripped, then the tip of the pencil broke.

Dejected, he threw the notebook and what was left of the pencil on the floor at my feet.

"This is ridiculous," I said with a sigh as Finley lay back onto his bed, curling up in the fetal position. His cheeks were flushed, and he looked ready to cry.

I knew I was running out of time and didn't have many options. Besides the dagger, the only other idea that came to mind was turning to Guy. Since he'd brought back my brother, he seemed willing to help in some strange way. But I didn't know how to find him. After his last visit, I'd told him in a not so amicable way not to come back, and who knew if he'd listen to me this time? I couldn't just wait around hoping he'd ignore me too.

Then I thought of the busty brunette he'd been with the first time—Lisbon. It seemed she was still attending classes, maybe helping to sneak Guy on and off campus. She'd probably be my best option given the limited time I had.

I still thought of involving Devon, but I'd gotten enough of my friends in trouble. I couldn't involve any more. And I still couldn't risk him turning me in. This could be way outside of his comfort zone of keeping secrets from his mother. Not to mention, she knew about my hidden crystal and I still didn't know how. She obviously had special means of getting information, and I didn't yet know what they were. I couldn't get Devon involved now.

I was on my own.

Lisbon seemed to be my best lead. However, unfortunately for me, I hadn't seen her all trimester besides the incident in my room on day one.

So, I set out on a mission to find her, starting by staking out the cafeteria morning, noon, and night. Everyone had to eat. I didn't let Nym in on what I was doing, wanting to keep her out of this. It was still possible the headmistress would use her as leverage for any of my future infractions, but I thought I could negotiate if Nym truly was no longer involved. So, with that, I distanced myself from her and the rest of my friends, citing a lot of extra work to catch up on.

Nym saw through that excuse, but assumed it was a rift forming between us at the loss of Razielle. I said it wasn't, but kept my demeanor somber, so it seemed true, but I didn't want to admit it. Whatever worked. I didn't want her to share the same fate as Razielle.

I'd talked with Razielle several times since she'd left, and she was pissed, but luckily, she wasn't pissed at me. She'd insisted on helping me, and accepted the risks. But that didn't mean she was going to roll over and take her expulsion without a fight. Her father—the archangel Raziel—was getting involved and supposed to appeal to some magical council. I wished her luck and the Academy wasn't the same without her.

On the third day of Operation All-Day Cafeteria, I finally saw Lisbon enter for breakfast. She was early, which was why I'd been missing her. But today, I arrived at 5:30, right when it opened. She had no intention of sitting down but grabbing a few food items and running.

Instead of confronting her in the cafeteria, I chased after her once she pushed through the doors. It was still only about 6 a.m., so the Academy grounds were mostly empty—all the non-mission-driven students still sleeping.

"Lisbon," I called after her, hurrying to catch up.

She immediately spun around, thrown off by the sound of her name in the early morning darkness. She looked about ready to attack until realizing it was me, then she just looked confused.

"What the hell do you want?" she asked. She was carrying a plastic container with an egg sandwich and assorted fruit in one hand and a coffee in the other.

"You're not an easy person to find." I stopped a few steps away from her. I'd taken nothing from the cafeteria.

"No one's supposed to be looking for me."

"Actually, I'm looking for Guy, but since I don't know how to get in touch with him, I thought you'd be the next logical choice."

"And what makes you think *I'll* help you?"

"Because I'm willing to say *please*?" I said with a hopeful smile. When she didn't immediately take the bait, I continued. "My brother needs help. You guys seem to care about him, otherwise you wouldn't have brought him back when he was in trouble."

"Guy can't do anything about the red thread," Lisbon said. "No one can. I'm sorry."

"Can you help me find him anyway?" I was desperate and sounded it.

"He was here like a week ago, but he must have gone back on his own because he didn't stop by before he left."

"Does he normally?"

"Normally I go with him."

"Back to Kicryria?"

"Him, not me," she said. "I've been told to stay here and make sure I remain in good standing." Lisbon began to walk again, forcing me to follow.

"How do I get there?" I asked.

"To Kicryria?"

"Yeah."

"You don't," Lisbon said with a laugh. "You don't know what you're asking. Guy may have a soft spot for you, but that doesn't mean I trust you."

"What are you talking about?" I scoffed. "He nearly murdered me. He held a gun to my head. I still think he coerced my little brother into stealing my needle."

"That was mostly your brother's idea. Guy actually wanted to invite you into the group, but your brother was adamantly against it. Not that I blame him. You do seem like an attention whore."

"Excuse me?" I was ready to go off on this bitch but had to quickly rein in my anger. I couldn't allow my eagerness to jump into a fight derail my mission and burn down the only bridge I currently had access to.

Lisbon shrugged like she didn't care one way or the other. "I'm just telling you how it went down. Believe what you want."

"Guy said he had a hand in what my brother did to me."

"Yeah, but that doesn't mean he initiated it."

"Fine; so, my brother's the asshole, not Guy," I said.

"I never said that." Lisbon laughed again. She also picked up her pace, headed back to the Manor. I was afraid I was going to lose her.

"What can I do to earn your trust?" I asked. "I just want one meeting with Guy."

"I don't know. I'm just looking out for myself right now. I don't need the extra trouble. I can't afford to lose my standing here." Lisbon suddenly stopped and turned to me. "And if you even think about trying to blackmail me, I'll make sure you—"

"I'm not gonna blackmail you," I interrupted. Then I reached into my pocket and pulled out the queen I'd been carrying around.

"What's that?" she asked.

"A Kicryrian totem," I said. "I stole it from the headmistress."

"You did what? Are you mental?"

"I think so," I said. "But regardless, this is my token of good faith to you. I was trying to get my hands on the Seam Dagger in Professor Voltaire's office, but that plan failed."

"The dagger in the case is a decoy," Lisbon said, smugly. "The real one is securely locked away."

"You don't say," I said, shaking my head, almost embarrassed I'd ever thought that heist would be so easy.

"I don't know of anyone naïve enough to try to steal it."

"Finding this amusing?"

"Yeah; actually, I am." She took a sip from her coffee since it was probably getting cold while we were chatting outside. "That's got to be one of the craziest and stupidest things I've heard in a long while."

"And it's probably not even in the top five of the craziest and stupidest things I've done," I said.

Lisbon's gaze drifted past me, then turned upward. "I heard you jumped out of the tower to save your boyfriend," she said.

I followed her gaze, realizing she could see the lonely stone tower from where she stood. "Yeah... well, that may have topped the list as the craziest thing I've ever done. But, hey—I lived to tell the tale."

"Guy was pretty impressed by that."

"Nothing says true love quite like jumping out of a twenty-story window for someone."

Lisbon took another sip of her coffee, her attention still off in the distance. "I can't believe I'm doing this. Okay, Maeve. I'll help you."

I couldn't believe it either. I'd somehow turned the conversation around and she was agreeing to get me in touch with Guy. With so many things going wrong, something was bound to go my way sooner or later. "Thank you," I said, trying not to sound too excited. I needed to maintain at least some semblance of control.

"Don't make me regret it," she warned.

CHAPTER 30

*D*evon rushed over to my room when I called even though it was still the middle of the night.

Finley woke up in a panic, unable to breathe. The sounds coming from him were animalistic as he coughed with a closed mouth and did everything he could to breathe through his nose. But he'd developed a cold over the past day and it had now completely taken over his nose.

He was nearly turning blue by the time I realized what was going on. I ran over to the desk, grabbed the smoothie straw and pushed it through his cheek to create an opening to allow him to breathe through his mouth.

His chest was heaving, his eyes wide with fear.

"You're going to be okay," I said, pulling him in for a hug. Even with everything Lisbon had said, I

MICHAEL PIERCE

still didn't want to believe Finley would have betrayed me on purpose. And I was going to hold onto my story for as long as possible.

Devon arrived a few minutes later, expecting an attack or a dead body. I hadn't explained the issue over the phone.

"I've temporarily alleviated the problem," I said. "But Finley developed a head cold and he can't breathe through his nose, which means he can't breathe, period. I've used the straw for now. There has to be something you can do."

Devon physically calmed, taking in a deep breath —almost rubbing it in. "You nearly gave me a heart attack," he said.

"It was an emergency," I said, leaving my brother's side. "You should have seen him before I thought to use the straw." I pictured what Devon had done for me back at my apartment—mostly fixing my nose. I didn't want anyone else coming in here, so it had to be Devon.

"The straw was good thinking," he said. "Finley, are you good for the moment?"

Finley nodded, holding the straw to his cheek, his breathing making a slight whistling sound.

"Good. Lie down and I'll see what I can do about clearing up your nose. It won't be perfect, but you should be able to breathe on your own by the time I'm done. Maeve, can you get me a wet face cloth?"

I dug a face cloth out of my wardrobe and wet it

using a bottled water. Finley was lying down when I handed it to Devon, who took a seat beside my brother.

I stood impatiently as Devon draped the cloth over Finley's face and applied pressure over his nose. He concentrated for a moment, then glanced up at me.

"Do you mind?" he asked and gestured for me to back up.

"What about all the stuff with focusing through distractions?" I argued, wanting to remain close to my brother.

"Do you really want me distracted right now?"

Pouting, I backed up and dropped into my desk chair.

Devon closed his eyes and went back to concentrating on the task at hand. Before I knew it, steam began to rise from the wet face cloth, so much so I was afraid it might catch fire. But I had to trust Devon knew what he was doing, so I bit down the urge to say or do anything.

It seemed to be taking so much longer than the work he'd done on me. I kicked my leg uncontrollably, then played with the buttons of my flannel pajamas to distract myself. At least I didn't have to worry about these pajamas distracting Devon. They were warm and comfy and not at all alluring.

While my thoughts jumped wildly from one thing to another, Devon brought my attention back to the present by removing the steaming cloth from Finley's face. The steam wasn't as thick as it had been before. Devon used the cloth to wipe his hands, seeming to relish the warmth the material was still giving off.

"How do you feel now?" he asked.

Finley slowly sat up and sniffled. Then he removed the straw from his cheek, the hole quickly closing, and sniffled again. Moments later, a smile formed on his gaunt face and he nodded.

"Good. I don't know exactly how long it will last, but I'll check on you tomorrow and can repeat the process as necessary to clear your sinuses."

Finley gave Devon another nod before sinking back into his bed and pulling up the covers.

"Thank you," I said. "Sorry if I was a little over-dramatic."

"I'm here to help," Devon said, giving me one of his star-studded, irresistible smiles. "I guess I'll head back to bed."

"Keep your phone close in case I need you again," I said, returning the smile.

"I always do." He leaned in and gave me a warm kiss. When our lips parted, he looked me up and down, his brilliant blue eyes radiating hunger. "You missed a button," he said.

"What?" I glanced down to check each and every one, instantly reminded of how I'd called out Erik. "No, I didn't."

Devon reached out and unhooked the top button on my pajama shirt. "There. That's better." He flashed a wicked grin, then wished Finley and me goodnight before leaving us to get some more sleep.

I left the top button undone as I crawled into bed, closed my eyes, and pictured that disarming and dangerous smile. I'd jumped out a window for him... and even after everything that had happened, I'd probably do it again.

DEVON PERFORMED the same magical procedure several times over the next few days until Finley finally got better.

During that time, I was also getting nervous that I hadn't heard from Lisbon about setting up a meeting with Guy. She was supposed to contact me when everything had been set up, but it had been radio silence for three days. I was afraid of the head-mistress finding out about the queen swap and coming for me. And if that happened, I could prob-ably kiss this place goodbye. But it wouldn't only be me. It would be Finley and Nym, and any connec-tion I still had with the souls of my parents.

On the fourth day, I showed up at the cafeteria before opening and waited. I waited until it was time for Morality of Magic to start, then headed off to class. For all I knew, Lisbon could be looking out for me now—actively avoiding me because she'd had second thoughts about helping or something else had gone wrong. I tried not to read too much into it and accept the waiting as a natural process.

The mood was still somber in Lab without Razielle. Our entire group dynamic wasn't the same without her. Even though it was hard to tell for outsiders, Nym was taking it the hardest, really reverting into her shell. I wished I could be there to better support her, but still felt it was safer to distance myself from her for now. And it hurt.

Nym wasn't even eating with the others anymore. Neither was I, for the most part. So, the group had essentially been reduced to Ivanic, Erik, Sarah, and Bree. Devon had me pair with Nym since her partner was gone, so he went back to rotating through the pairs to see what we needed the most help with.

Nym was still struggling with Non-Magical Studies, where I could assist her. On the other hand, I was falling behind in Supernatural History because I couldn't concentrate on all the reading and memo-rization. I was still passing, so there wasn't a threat of me failing the class. I was just hovering at a solid C. There were worse things.

"I feel bad for Nym," Devon said once everyone else had left for dinner. "I know no one wants to talk about Razielle's exit, but they'd become so close in a strange, bickering sisters sort of way."

I hadn't opened up to him about what had

happened to Razielle, so I didn't know how much information he was privileged to—how much his mother was spilling at their kitchen table or over a game of chess—or whatever it was they did together.

"She'll be fine," I said. "They still talk."

"And you know that?"

"Yeah," I said. "I talk to her too."

"Do you want to talk about it?" Devon asked, leaning forward in our facing desks to take my hands.

I shook my head. "What's done is done. It sucks and we need to move on."

"That's like your whole life philosophy, isn't it?"

"What is?"

"Suppress what sucks and move on with your life."

"I don't suppress shit," I said. "I just don't dwell on it. Dwelling makes you crazy. My brother does that, and it really gets under his skin. So, yeah, I don't dwell and move on."

"I just want us to be open and honest with each other," Devon said, rubbing circles along the backs of my hands. "Relationships don't work long term otherwise."

"You know what? You've never talked about a previous relationship."

"Neither have you, expect for that Ben guy."

"He wasn't a relationship. He was—*is* a longtime friend," I said. "But don't dodge my question."

"You didn't ask me a question." Devon smirked like he'd checkmated me.

I had to think for a moment to recall what I'd specifically said. I sighed. "Urgh... Fine, Mr. Literal. What was your last relationship like? When. How long. What screwed it up. All that kinda stuff."

"Only if you'll do the same."

"Sure," I agreed, knowing I didn't have much to say. I didn't have much experience in the relationship department. I'd moved around so much, just when I felt I was getting to know someone, my life was uprooted yet again. So, I stopped trying and just started keeping things physical and casual.

"My last relationship lasted nearly three years," Devon started. "I'd met her in the second trimester of my first year. She was a medial, came from a well-to-do family of shifters, and we clicked from the very beginning."

"What was her name?"

"Clara. She was a white wolf shifter from the Canadian Rockies. Her hair was as white as the snow. She became my whole world. Since she was a year ahead of me, she helped me out with my abilities and helped get me through some classes. When she became a Master Classman, she became a coach, like I am now. She took her job really seriously. It's a great privilege and honor. Fewer than twenty percent of us get the opportunity."

"I'm sure your mother had nothing to do with it for you," I said, smirking.

Devon let go of my hands. "Why do you do that?"

"Do what?"

"Keep assuming I get everything handed to me."

"Don't you? Of course, the others don't know."

"I work hard for everything I get." Devon's eyes furrowed as he glared at me. "I earn my opportunities."

"I'm sure you do, but don't you think your family position plays at least a small role in some of that decision making? I'm not judging you. I say take advantage of every opportunity at your disposal. If I were in your shoes, I'd do the same thing."

Devon pumped his jaw and sat there with a sulky expression. It was obviously a sore subject to imply his status awarded him opportunities, earned or not.

"I'm sorry," I said. "I didn't mean to piss you off. It started off as a joke, then I took it too far like I usually do. So, getting back to your story, what happened between you two?"

Devon gave me a look like he didn't want to continue, but after a sullen pause, he finally did. "With her upcoming graduation, we talked about our future. I only had one more year and Clara was looking at different universities. She finally settled on one in Quebec, then started voicing her fears of a long-distance relationship. In the position we're in, long distance doesn't really apply. It became obvious she didn't want to start a new school tied down—she wanted a fresh start. So shortly after graduation, she broke up with me."

"Just like that?"

"Just like that," he said, like the situation was still painful. "I've kept in touch with her. We speak from time to time, but we're different people now."

"Have you told her about me?" I asked.

Devon shook his head. "That would just feel awkward."

"I suppose so."

"What about you? What's your most recent relationship?" Devon slid his hands back over to my desk, maneuvering them back into mine.

"I don't think I've ever been in a relationship long enough to call it one," I said.

"That's it? After everything I just told you, that's all you're gonna give me?"

"You know I moved around a lot. It taught me not to get too close to people. I befriended the kids in my group homes, but never dated any. Other kids were naturally drawn to me at school—to my brashness mostly—but I kept them at an arm's length. I had reoccurring hookups, but I'm sure you don't want to hear about those. That was the most I could give. I needed to be strings-free too."

"What's changed?" Devon asked, expectantly.

"I don't know," I said. "Maybe I'm growing up. Maybe I've finally found my home. Maybe I've taken so many risks here, this one feels like a natural progression." I didn't want to say that maybe the crystals had set us up to a point where I didn't even know which feelings were mine.

"So, I'm like your first," he said with a devilishly sly grin, squeezing my hands.

"It depends on what you mean by that," I said. "You're a little late to pop my cherry."

"Yeah, and I don't think many virgins would put it like that."

I smiled and shrugged. "You should know by now what you've gotten yourself into."

"I do," he said, then stood up still holding my hand and guided me out of the desk chair. He pulled me into him and suddenly his lips were on mine, fervent and fierce.

I was so desperate to stave off the mounting stress of everything in my life that I was finally ready to commit to the moment—commit to Devon here and now. And I could feel he wanted it too.

He pushed me back into the next desk and I hopped up onto it, pulling him in and wrapping my legs around his waist as we continued to hungrily feed off each other. His lips left mine as he trailed kisses down my neck, licking and nibbling. When he worked his way back up, he took my earlobe in his mouth and playfully grazed my skin with his teeth. A soft moan escaped my lips as he continued to work through my accessible skin. Then he went for more.

My mind went back to him unbuttoning my pajama shirt, wishing my brother hadn't been there and Devon not having to stop at just one button, with nothing between his deft hands and my tingling skin but the soft layer of cotton.

Today, I had no buttons to slowly work and heighten the anticipation. Devon grabbed the bottom of my shirt and tugged it up and over my head, then tossed the discarded garment onto the adjacent desk. I had on a tank top underneath, which I was about to remove when I glanced over at the door.

"There's a window in the door," I said. I'd locked it, but there wasn't much I could do about the glass. There wasn't a shade to pull down.

Devon stared at the window for a long moment, all the while his hands gripping the outsides of my thighs. I leaned in to kiss his neck while he was focused on the door.

"Done," he said.

When his eyes returned to me, I had to take another look over my shoulder, discovering the glass had somehow been blacked out, eliminating the fear of someone peeking in and catching us in the act.

My tank top was tucked into my jeans and Devon was actively searching for the bottom of it. Instead of risking him tearing one of my few good tank tops, I batted his hands away, then unbuttoned my jeans, reached inside, and found the bottom of the tank top. Devon helped me pull it off, and before he got me naked while he was still fully clothed, I made sure to level the playing field.

Once we dropped enough clothing to the floor, we reached the point of no return, already a tangle of limbs, lips, and unbridled libidos. And it was everything I'd hoped it would be. Everything I'd needed—at least for the moment.

Afterward, still lost in each other's arms, naked and sweating, all the stress from before came flooding back, but at least I didn't feel quite so alone. Maybe it was time to truly give this relationship thing a try. Maybe it was time to let someone else in for real.

CHAPTER 31

Despite the stress of not hearing a peep from Lisbon, I was all smiles the next day. I couldn't wipe that silly fucking grin off my face. And when Devon texted me about how amazing the previous evening had been—and actually called me his girlfriend—I had proof besides my sore core muscles that it hadn't been a crazy ass dream. Yeah; it had been a while.

Am I supposed to, like, officially meet his mother now?

I cringed at the thought, though the glued-on grin didn't falter.

I wanted to have lunch with the gang today and invited Nym to join. At first, she refused, but I wore her down. We got our food and found Ivanic and Bree already seated at one of the tables.

"Well, this is a nice surprise," Ivanic said as we sat down across from them.

"Hey, guys," Bree said after sipping her iced tea. "You sure look like you're in a good mood today." That comment was obviously aimed at me.

"You *do* look happy," Ivanic seconded. "That's so unlike you. There's usually a scowl on your face."

"There is not," I argued.

"Wait a sec… did you get some?"

My cheeks burned with a heightened smile that I couldn't suppress. I didn't even have to say anything.

"I knew it!" Ivanic exclaimed, though I couldn't quite tell the tone.

"Who got some?" Sarah asked as she approached the table with Erik.

"Maeve did, apparently," Bree said. It was clear she didn't want to hear about it.

Shit, maybe it was a mistake coming here today.

"Is it appropriate to say *nice job* to a girl?" Erik asked.

"No," Sarah said.

"As a rule, I'd agree," I said. "But I'll take it."

"This isn't over," Ivanic said. "Devon may have you for now, but he won't have you for good. You're too good for him."

"As always, I appreciate the concern," I said. "But *please* don't wait around for me. Sow your wild oats —or whatever it is cougars do."

"I need to remain vigilant, so I don't miss the moment when you need me to come and rescue you."

I laughed. "Now I know you're talking to the wrong girl. I don't and *will not* need rescuing."

"Then maybe you'll rescue *me,* and my vulnerability will change the tide of our relationship and make you finally fall madly in love with me," Ivanic said.

"There's no convincing you, is there?" I asked, still laughing.

Ivanic flashed a debonair smile and shrugged. "I just know, even if you don't yet."

The conversation finally drifted to other things, sparing me more of Ivanic's delusional life view. Bree seemed a little peeved, so I wanted to smooth that over too. Nym didn't say much, but it meant a lot to have her here and included with the group.

After most of us had finished our food, I felt a presence behind me and noticed as those on the other side of the table became intrigued by someone. Before I could turn around, there was a tap on my shoulder.

I turned to the figure standing over me only to find a large rack directly in my face. I didn't have to raise my eyelevel to know who it was.

"Maeve, can we talk?" Lisbon asked.

"Of course," I said and stood with my empty tray. "I'll catch you guys later."

Both guys were gawking at the voluptuous wonder that was Lisbon. Sarah and Bree were sizing her up too. Then Sarah smacked Erik in the arm to bring him out of his boobilicious siren trance.

Lisbon didn't want to talk in the cafeteria, so she led me outside into the cold. I zipped up my leather jacket and retrieved my gloves from the pockets. She continued to walk me away from the cafeteria before saying anything.

"I thought you'd forgotten about me," I said, trying to break the ice.

"I've been trying to get a hold of Guy," she said, finally stopping where there weren't any other students nearby.

"And from the look on your face, you don't have good news."

"I'm concerned that he left that last time without talking to me and now he seems to be MIA," Lisbon said. "You said you saw him. How did that conversation go?"

"It wasn't exactly pleasant because I was kinda pissed about him randomly showing up in my room," I said, then remembered Guy disappearing when I'd been distracted by the soul crystal in Finley's hand. I'd chased after him all the way outside, but he was gone like a vampire in sunlight. "He left suddenly, and when I went to look for him, he'd vanished."

"He has a way of doing that," Lisbon said. "One of his many gifts. So, I don't know what's up with him.

But you'd wanted him to help you get to Kicryria, right?"

"That was the ultimate plan," I said.

"A stupid plan, if you ask me. But if that's where you really want to go, then I can help you get there."

"Really?" I was beyond excited. Nervousness hadn't set in yet, but I was sure it would soon enough.

"Yeah, but I want you to do something for me first," Lisbon said.

"Name it."

"I'm sure your boyfriend is able to get some insider information. Ask him to inquire about Guy. I want to rule out the possibility of him being captured or worse. See what you can find out."

"Okay," I said, not exactly sure how I was going to accomplish that. "When will you help me get to Kicryria?"

"After you get the final word from your boyfriend."

"And what if it's bad news?"

"We'll cross that bridge when we come to it," Lisbon said, which I interpreted to mean, *then the deal's off.*

"Can I get your number, so it doesn't take me another four days to find you?"

Lisbon almost seemed reluctant, like she'd be giving up her power if she did so. But in the end, she complied, and we exchanged numbers.

. . .

Devon knew that Guy had been back to the Academy to drop off Finley, but I hadn't told him that Guy had made a return visit. So, the only way I could think to spin the story was with my concern that he was still out there and if Devon could look into it.

Did anyone know anything? Had anyone else seen him?

Within a few hours, Devon got back to me saying there was no sign of Guy on Academy grounds, but the guards were on alert. He assured me I had nothing to worry about—except I wasn't really worried about Guy.

I didn't want Finley to hear my plan—not that he was in a position to do anything about it—so I went outside to call Lisbon. I'd actually be talking to her twice in one day.

"Well, I take that as good news," she said after I'd relayed the information received from Devon. "Maybe he was sent on a blackout mission or something."

"Are we still on?" I asked.

The other end of the line was silent for a long moment, to where I thought I might have lost reception. Then she broke the radio silence with a clipped, "Yeah."

I waited to see if she'd elaborate, but she didn't. "When?" I pressed.

More silence.

Is she checking her goddamn calendar?

"I'm tired tonight," Lisbon finally said. "We'll do it tomorrow. Meet me in the village square at midnight."

"I'll be there," I said.

There were no more pleasantries. Lisbon simply hung up. I paced around in the snow for another ten minutes before going back inside and getting ready for bed. Tomorrow was going to be a long day and I needed to be well rested.

CHAPTER 32

I texted Lisbon before heading down to the village. She didn't answer, but I left the comfort of my room anyway. I was quiet not to wake Finley, planning to be back by sunup.

I didn't know what I'd expected to find in Kicryria, but I needed to see it for myself. That would be the first step. Maybe I'd be able to find Guy there, and he'd help me get the needle or my parents' crystals back. Something where I didn't feel like I was going home empty handed.

I thought back to the opportunity I'd had to enter the seam in my apartment and how terrifying the thought had been. I couldn't bring myself to do it. Now I *had* to.

I'd conquered my fear of the dark at a young age, but never really liked it. I wanted to be in control— and control meant knowing what was in front of me.

I had no idea what was on the other side of the seam, and that was becoming more terrifying by the second.

I walked through the Academy gates and into the village with my trusty Docs and leather jacket. They made up my superhero outfit—my armor. I didn't have a crystal anymore to amplify my powers; all I had left were the items that had given me power since before I'd known magic existed.

When I reached the square, I didn't see a single soul in the dim light. Many of the lights were turned off at this hour, only a fraction remaining to illuminate the entire village. I headed to one of the many empty tables and pulled out a chair. The metal legs against the concrete screeched and could probably have woken the dead.

I checked my phone as I sat down, confirming I was right on time. And there was still no return text. I sat and shivered in the dark, wondering if this was all a big joke—if Lisbon had set me up and had no intention of helping me get to Kicryria. But before I could be completely consumed by thoughts of doubt, I noticed two figures approaching from the Academy.

The dim light of the square made it hard to recognize them from afar, but as they drew closer, I realized it was indeed Lisbon—as well as a guy I'd seen once before.

"Maeve?" Lisbon called into the night.

"Yeah," I answered and stood to greet them.

"This is Storm. He's a friend and can help you navigate over there."

I glanced at the large guy I briefly remembered being introduced to in the cafeteria last trimester. His hair was dark and unruly, longer than I remembered from last time, now falling into his eyes. He was in a black flannel long-sleeved shirt, obviously impervious to the cold. The shirt wasn't even that thick because I could see his crystal glowing from beneath it.

"He's coming with me?" I asked Lisbon.

"Yes," Storm said in an impossibly low voice.

"I don't need an escort," I said, sounding like a petulant child. I knew I probably did because I had no freakin' clue what I was going to do when I got there, but I didn't know this Storm guy at all. He'd be in control, and that bothered me.

"What, are you just going to navigate through the compass on your phone?" Lisbon asked, sounding amused. "Oh, wait, your phone isn't going to work over there. I guess you'll have to go old school and navigate by the stars. Oh, wait, the stars are totally different too. That's okay, you can just follow the signs. Oh. Wait. If only you could read the language."

"Okay; you proved your point," I said. "I appreciate you thinking ahead on my behalf."

"So, do we all have the warm and fuzzies and feel ready to go? Or did I stay up this late for nothing?"

MICHAEL PIERCE

"I'm good," I said. "Lead the way."

Storm had only said the one word since they'd arrived, and he didn't start casual conversation as Lisbon led us past the square and farther into Spellcrest Village. The quaint stores soon became quaint townhomes as we continued down the foggy street. After a few turns, we slipped between two buildings and snuck around to the back of a townhome.

Lisbon dropped to her knees and grabbed a rock from under a stretch of bushes. Then she returned to her feet, stone in hand, and approached the back door.

"Are you seriously going to break a window with that th—" But as I was asking the question, I saw the large rock shrink in her hands, then transform into a key.

I guess that's how they hide the key in the fake rock in magic land—hide the key as the rock.

"Ye of little faith," Lisbon said and unlocked the back door of the dark townhome. Storm snorted a laugh as the two of them proceeded inside, leaving me in the frigid midnight air.

The inside of the townhome was completely empty—no furniture, no pictures, and no electricity. The only things left behind from the previous residents were the appliances and curtains.

"What *is* this place?" I asked.

"It's where we keep the unlocked door," Lisbon said, using her phone for light, now crouching by the wall next to the fireplace. "You won't need that totem of yours." She lifted the edge of the carpet and pulled out what looked like a phone charging cord. It didn't stretch that far, so she had to remain close to the ground to plug in her phone and dial someone's number.

When I drew closer to her, I noticed the cord wasn't plugged into an outlet in the wall, but the cord itself disappeared into the wall.

"Who used to live here?" I asked as Lisbon held her phone to her ear.

"Otis," Storm said. "The Academy got rid of his stuff fast after what happened last year. Now it's for sale."

"So, if this is like your secret hideout, aren't you going to lose it?"

"We're here," Lisbon said, promptly hung up, then turned her attention to me. "We're working on getting a friendly buyer to keep it within our control."

"And if you can't?" I asked.

"Then we build a new door," Lisbon said, rolling her eyes. "Seems like that would be obvious."

"I don't know," I shot back. "I'm still trying to figure out what's going on here."

Before the argument could continue, I noticed the wall begin to split apart like sliding doors at a supermarket. A vertical line opened and widened in the wall from the floor to about six feet up. The new lines in the wall shimmered like the few seams I'd seen before, only darkness visible within. Criss-crossing red thread stretched across the seam in the wall like a bloody spiderweb. The opening stopped widening at about two feet, the thread still spanning the entire opening.

"We have to move fast," Lisbon said. "If the seam is left open for more than a minute or so, it will become detectable to the seamstresses—primarily the headmistress. A quick open and close will only register as a glitch or a natural anomaly. Have fun, you guys. I'll be heading back to bed."

"Thank you," I said. "Your help means more than you know."

"Maybe I *do* know," she said with a smirk and gestured for Storm to go first—to show me the way. "Be careful of the thread. You don't want to dislodge any of the incision points."

I nodded and watched Storm maneuver through the crisscrossing thread as if he was tackling an obstacle course. As each part of his body passed the thread and entered the seam, it was swallowed in the void between the shimmering edges.

As much as I had been in Ben's apartment, I was afraid of what lay beyond the seam—what world I'd truly be stepping into. But Lisbon didn't give me any time for hesitation. I had ten seconds to get my ass into the void or it would be closed.

So, I got my ass into the void.

CHAPTER 33

*T*he thread felt like trip wires as I carefully made my way through without snapping anything. I knew the thread wouldn't break. As I'd seen with Finley's lips, the thread seemed to be unbreakable. But supposedly, it could rip through the universal fabric and keep the seam from closing entirely. If it didn't close entirely, then it would be picked up on the headmistress's radar, which was what we *didn't* want to happen.

As I stepped through the seam, the black void turned into blinding light. I had to close my eyes and take the last step into Kicryria on faith.

"Can you go any slower?" a voice asked—a voice that sounded oddly familiar, but I couldn't place it with my eyes closed. And it sure wasn't Storm's. It was a girl's voice. "We have to close this thing before you blow our cover."

A strong hand grabbed my arms and yanked me to one side. At first, I didn't know if I was being helped or captured. So, I pushed through the pain of the light to squint and take inventory of my immediate surroundings.

Storm had been the one to grab my arm and haul me away from the open seam. He let go once I was out of the way.

As I squinted, my eyes adjusted and quickly landed on the back of a girl with long black hair approaching the open seam. She knelt before the shimmering doorway and picked up a spool of thread on the ground. After wrapping a length of thread around her hand, she began to tug, and as she did so, the opening steadily closed. Within seconds, the seam had disappeared—the wall fused back together. The girl wound the extra thread onto the spool and placed it back onto the floor by the wall. One end of the thread still disappeared into the wall, and at the entry point, I noticed another—or more likely, the other side of the phone cord.

"That's crazy," I said, rubbing my eyes to help get them fully adjusted. "You don't need a needle or dagger."

"We needed a needle originally to set this up, but now it can be maintained without outside supplies," the girl said, then turned around—letting me know exactly why her voice had sounded familiar.

"Holy shit, it's you!" I said.

"Yeah; it's a small universe," Quin said—the girl who'd stolen my blood in Ben's apartment!

There was no evidence I'd broken her nose previously, yet I so wanted to see what other damage I could inflict. I'd been so afraid of what she was doing with my blood, and here we were, together again.

"Don't do anything stupid," she said. "I can tell you're thinking about it."

"What did you do with my blood?" I demanded, taking an angry step closer to her.

She didn't flinch. "I don't need to explain it to you. You'll see for yourself soon enough. But before we get going, where's my Reese's?" Quin was looking past me, her gaze set on Storm.

"Oh, yeah," he said, reached into his pocket, and pulled out a Reese's Peanut Butter Cup, and tossed it to her.

"I love these things," she said, immediately ripping open the package and tossing one of the candy cups into her mouth. "Peanut butter fused with chocolate—who would've thought it? Right?"

"Umm… yeah, I guess. They're good," I said, not quite getting the extent of her fascination.

"Whenever I try to make them here, they're just not the same." Quin released a moan reminiscent of a small orgasm as she led us out of the house we'd stepped into.

I watched her as she ate her candy, picturing the

girl who'd broken into Ben's apartment, slicing open a seam right in the middle of the freakin' living room, which had also doubled as my bedroom at the time.

"Wait a sec," I said. "You said you'd been in my apartment for a long time when we'd shown up."

"Yeah…" Quin said, still munching on the Reese's.

"Then why was it such an emergency to close *this* seam so fast?"

Storm chuckled like I wasn't in on the joke.

Quin took a moment to finish chewing and swallowed before replying. "I had help with a cloaking spell that day because I didn't know how long I'd be waiting. I really wanted to avoid getting my ass kicked by the nearest seamstress, though you got in a few good punches too."

Damn right, I did.

It wasn't until we made our way toward the door that I noticed the house was in shambles. Random items were strewn about the floor. Furniture was fallen and broken. Windows were shattered, and sunlight poured in as thick diagonal pillars of dusty light.

"It's daytime?" I asked as Quin opened the front door, which was barely hanging by the hinges.

"Yeah; it's a little past noon. Our schedule is nearly opposite yours."

"What happened here?" I asked as we stepped into the warm afternoon sun—and *warm* was an understatement. It must have been at least eighty degrees, which I'd started to feel when we arrived, but it didn't fully hit me until we got outside. I surely didn't need my leather jacket here, but also didn't want to carry it, so I kept it on. It also explained why Quin was only in a blue tank top.

Once I got a good look around outside, I realized the full extent of my question. Every building in sight was in as bad or worse shape than the one we'd just left. Some buildings were nothing but wreckage. Others were less obviously destroyed, but still showed signs of distress.

"A massacre," Quin said without much emotion. "That's what happened here."

I didn't see any dead bodies, but as I looked more closely at the debris, I noticed what I thought was blood. There was little doubt people had died here. And this looked like a bigger town than the one we'd just left. Houses and other buildings stretched for at least several miles. And nothing appeared to have been spared. I read about war. I'd seen it on television. But I'd never seen the aftermath of it firsthand. It was eerie and quiet. The air was stuffy and thick, which only added to the heaviness of the desolated landscape.

"Welcome to Ogginosh." Quin maneuvered through the rubble-filled street. "What's left of it, anyway."

"Who did this?" I asked, falling behind as I

continued to take in the destruction—oddly high-lighted by the blazing sun. Somehow, I felt like it would appear less creepy at night, maybe because all the wretched details would remain hidden in darkness.

"You did. Well, not you, per se—but your people."

"We did this?" I couldn't believe it. Then I remembered hearing the name of the town before, tracking it back to the night in Ben's apartment, after Quin had left and I'd called for the head-mistress to sew up the seam. She'd said that name and was obviously familiar with it. Had it been in this state then? Or had this happened since that crazy night?

Storm kicked some rocks or chunks of broken buildings, creating a dust cloud he then walked through. He now had the sleeves of his flannel shirt rolled up past the elbows.

I glanced over at a store with a sign hanging from a chain on one side and realized what was written on it—from what could still be read—was in an alien language, like nothing I'd ever seen.

"We weren't here at the time," Quin said. "There wasn't much of a military presence here at all. So, when your soldiers arrived, they destroyed every-thing and took as many souls as they could find. Retaliation for the incident in Spellcrest not long ago, I'm sure. But it was still a low blow. We were able to rescue a few before your people took everyone. And once our military arrived, the members of your operation retreated quickly."

I still couldn't believe our people were responsible for this. And if they were, they must have had a better reason than just retaliation for what happened at Spellcrest. Yes, they'd killed two angels and it was horrific, but those angels were guards—warriors flying into battle. This—this was a town full of regular people if what Quin had explained was true.

"We're almost there," Quin said, turning onto another street in just as much disrepair as the one we'd left behind. "You probably didn't expect to need sunblock when you rolled out of bed in the middle of the night."

"Not at all," I said.

"And the ultraviolet rays are much harsher here than your world, so you'll burn quicker."

"Fantastic."

"It's actually not so bad. It's a very hostile environment for vampires to survive."

"Vampires exist too?" I asked, though I shouldn't have been surprised. Everything else seemed to be real, so why not vampires?

"My dad said you were a real newbie," Quin said, with a chuckle. "I didn't really believe it, especially after you got me pretty good in that apartment."

"You better still be planning on telling me what you did with my blood."

"*Relax.*" She sounded exasperated like *I* was the problem.

She was the one who'd stolen *my* blood to do God knew what with it. And I was the freakin' unreasonable one? I was also under the impression that the protection spell Professor Windsor had put on me wouldn't still be doing its job here. So yeah, it was a little hard to relax right now. If Storm wasn't walking directly beside me, I probably would have attacked her again. I knew she had some crazy powers too, but I'd risk it one on one.

How about I stab you *with a needle and tell you to relax. See how you like it.*

I needed to get my needle back. I wasn't sure how that was going to happen, but one step at a time was hopefully getting me closer. I was in Kicryria, reunited with the girl who'd taken my blood and I hadn't killed her yet. I didn't know who else we were going to meet, but was hopeful someone would help me—or at least point me in the right direction. I deserved to get my parents back. They belonged with Finley and me. And I needed the needle to free my brother from his un-vow of silence, as well as replenish the abilities I so dearly missed.

"Here we are," Quin finally said as she turned into what looked like a store with an apartment overhead. The buildings to the left and right had caved-in roofs, but this one seemed to still be intact, suffering minimal damage compared to its neighbors.

Quin opened the door and strolled in without pausing. I glanced over at Storm, who gestured for me to go ahead of him. I was afraid of the next surprise, but I'd already come this far. There was no way I was stopping now.

I peered up at the sign over the door, which was still complete gibberish, before entering the building. The inside seemed to be mostly gutted. What had been a store was furnished more like a living room and dining room. There were a number of people milling about, ranging in age from seven to seventy. The vibe in the room was as heavy as the air outside.

Quin was already approaching one group of solemn people. "I'm back. And we have company."

A seated man with slicked black hair facing away from the door slightly turned his head at the sound of her voice. Then he stood, gave her a warm hug, and searched out the new arrivals.

When he turned, my blood reached its boiling point from the mere sight of him. The loving greeting Quin had given him only fueled my rage.

"Maeve," Otis said, offering a conflicted smile. "I'm sure you have—"

"I should fucking kill you!" I roared. The thought of him holding me down while instructing Finley how to extract my needle made me see red. Ultimately, he was the reason I'd lost my needle. He'd betrayed everyone. I'd thought he was looking out for me from the beginning. But he'd been hiding a terrible personal agenda.

Otis threw his hands up in surrender. "There's no need for fighting. And after what these people have lived through, let's not joke about death."

"I'm not joking." I was ready to lunge for him when another voice instantly froze my boiling blood —then the sight of the woman who owned that voice as she stood a few feet past Otis.

"Maeve, my darling."

I couldn't move. I couldn't speak. If my legs supported me for one more second, it would be an absolute miracle. I couldn't believe my eyes. And all the emotions I'd been protecting beneath the thick skin built over the past ten years came rushing to the surface.

"Mom?"

CHAPTER 34

I remembered the last time I'd seen my mother. She'd dropped me off at 1st Grade on a typical Tuesday morning. It was June and gloomy, and the last week of school. I had on a pink hooded jacket, a skirt with built-in shorts, and Converse sneakers I could actually tie myself.

The bell had already rung, and we were running late. Mom parked in front of a house down the street and we rushed to my classroom. Well, she was rushing and I was taking my sweet-ass time, not feeling the urgency of time commitments yet. She held my hand and was practically dragging me down the street.

When we reached my classroom, she knelt to my level and we gave each other a great big hug.

"I love you, Mommy," I said.

"I love you more, my brave little Maeve," she said, stood, blew me a kiss, and walked away.

I walked into the room, hung my backpack on the hook, and found my desk. I said *hi* to my friends and went through a normal day, expecting to be picked up at 2:50. But she didn't show up. It wasn't until the school made some calls that everyone started to realize there was something wrong. My parents hadn't been found yet, but they were gone.

SEEING the vision of my mother now, she looked exactly the same—like I was seven years old again and she had finally arrived to pick me up from school.

In that moment, everything I'd learned about my parents and their secret lives disappeared. Later, I'd care and need some answers, but right now… none of that mattered.

I wanted to run to her and throw my arms around her beautiful body, but I was anchored to the spot in which I was currently standing. I didn't even know how I was still standing because I could no longer feel my legs. I was in shock, maybe even hysterical—and I didn't rule out the possibility of this moment being a sadistic hallucination.

"Oh my God, Maeve!" Mom cried and rushed over to me just as my legs gave way, catching me as I crumbled to the floor. She wrapped her arms around me and held me tight.

I felt arms around me—she was real. And as I lay my head on her shoulder I started to cry. It simply wasn't possible to hold in ten years of loss any longer. As she tightened her arms around me, the sobs only intensified. I couldn't get a single word out. I couldn't even think in terms of the present. Suddenly, I was her little girl again and never wanted to let her go for fear she might leave me again and never return.

"I'm here, my brave little Maeve—who's not quite so little anymore," she purred. "I can't believe how much you've grown in the blink of an eye, yet I'd still be able to recognize you anywhere."

"Y—you look e—exactly the same," I managed to get out between sobs. "I don't u—understand. How're you here?"

Mom forced my head off her shoulder and wiped my cheeks with her thumbs. As she did so, she looked directly into my eyes and smiled. "I love you," she said. "I want you to always know that—you and your brother. Whatever happens now, know that I've always loved the both of you. I've made mistakes, but I'm only human. I've paid for my mistakes—and I'm sure I'll continue to pay for them. But never question my devoted love for the two of you."

"How are you here?" I repeated, still unable to

fully comprehend how she had materialized before me.

"Your sacrifice gave me new life," she said, beaming even brighter than before.

"What does that mean? What sacrifice?"

"Necromancers are able to transport the souls from crystals into new bodies. That's widely known in the magic community, even back on earth. What isn't so well known is the ability to transport someone into a new body and transform that body into a carbon copy of the original using blood from a close relative."

"My blood…"

"Exactly."

I located Quin standing in the background. "That was your intention all along? You weren't trying to clone me or turn me into some suicide bomber puppet?"

"What? God no," Quin scoffed. "What do you take us for?"

"I—I have no freakin' clue." I turned back to Mom. "So, my blood that the girl over there jacked brought you back as yourself?"

"New and improved," she said with a chuckle. "Not exactly the same because your DNA also has your father's code, but close enough. I can see the differences, but I'm just being picky." Mom stood and offered me her hand.

My legs were still shaky, but I was able to get to

my feet. I glanced around at everyone in the room staring at us. There must have been at least twenty people. Typically, being the center of attention didn't bother me much—but I typically wasn't crying in front of large groups of people, either. I typically wasn't crying in front of *anyone*... However, this was about as far from a typical freakin' day as one could get.

"Why didn't you tell me what was going on?" I asked Quin.

"Ask my father," she said and jabbed her thumb in Otis's direction.

"That son of a bitch is your father?"

"Maeve, *language*," Mom scolded like she was still in charge of me. Yeah; she hadn't been around to witness the evolution of the explosive person I was today.

I should have deduced that Otis was Quin's father when she'd hugged him upon arrival, but there hadn't been much time to process that revelation with my mother popping out of thin air.

"Sorry," I said, then added, "But he is," under my breath.

"No comment," Quin said, giving a sly smile, as she'd obviously heard my remark.

"Your mother is still weak," Otis said, coming closer and stopping next to her. It seemed he thought she'd keep him safe from me. "And we didn't want to get your hopes up. The success rate for this kind of thing isn't high and we might have lost her entirely."

"So, you risked her soul on an experimental procedure that could have... What could it have done exactly if it failed? Obliterated her soul? Eternal damnation?"

"No—nothing like that," Otis laughed, but stopped himself when he saw the seriousness of my expression. "The worst that would have happened was her soul being set free. Not terrible for her at all."

"But *I* would have lost her," I said.

"You didn't have her to begin with."

"She'd been with me for months and I felt the connection. I felt the love. I may not have known it was her—but she was a part of me."

"And I always will be," Mom said, pulling me in for another hug. "I can't believe what a beautiful young woman you've become."

"You couldn't see me from inside the crystal?"

"I could, but... it's different."

"I know it doesn't mean much now, but I'm sorry for what happened," Otis said. "It was important..." He stopped after a warning look from my mother.

"What was that?" I asked.

"Nothing," Mom said.

"No more fucking secrets," I said.

"Maeve!"

"*Sorry!* But seriously, I can't take anymore fu—

secrets. Every day I learn some new detail about life or *my* life that totally jacks with my entire world-view. It's exhausting."

"There will be time for all of it," Mom said.

Then the most obvious question came to me. "What about Dad? Where is he?" I didn't like the crestfallen looks from everyone in the near vicinity. "What? What's wrong?"

"He's no longer in our possession," Otis said.

"Then, where is he?"

"Tarquin Drome—you might remember him as the—"

"Yeah; I remember that freaky bastard," I said. "He's like an Elite Special Forces something-or-other. He killed those two angels in the tower. He killed Helena. He killed Devon's father. And he stole my needle and sewed my brother's mouth shut—which under normal circumstances might have been an improvement. I'm familiar with the guy, and it's one of the main reasons I'm here."

"He's also claimed your father's crystal for himself," Otis said. "He's as lost as your needle."

"My needle's not lost," I said. "Tarquin has it. We know exactly where it is. Now I just need to get it back, with or without your help."

"Maeve dear, you don't understand who this man really is," Mom said. "He is in charge of the Elite Forces and reports to the general of the Kicryrian army. I may not know much of what happened in the past ten years, but I know the attack against our seam was no coincidence. I know we were set up."

"You don't know that," Otis said.

"He wanted Peter's position and he got it," Mom said, raising her voice. "We were eliminated by our own soldiers."

"Tarquin wanted Dad's position?" I asked.

Mom nodded. "We had the seam successfully cloaked for months. Tarquin had always been a threat and your father was about to report him for extreme insubordination. It was important to your father to use the proper chain of command. Tarquin moved out and took some of the guys more loyal to him. We were literally ambushed the next day. It was *not* a coincidence."

"Then it's more important to be careful now, more than ever," Otis said.

"There are soldiers approaching," a woman said, positioned by a front window. She wasn't someone I knew, but she also spoke perfect English.

"Move quickly!" Otis said. "Everyone in the basement! Move! Move!"

All the people who'd been lounging around jumped up and were now running for their lives toward a set of stairs where Quin was holding the door open.

"Hide. Quickly now," she said, ushering everyone down the stairs.

Mom grabbed my hand and led me toward the stairs as well, but I pulled back.

"Is that *him* coming?" I asked, feeling the fury return.

"I don't know, but we don't want to take any chances," she said.

Otis appeared at my side. "You need to hide with the others. Both of you. He'll kill you both on sight."

"So, it *is* him?"

Otis nodded. "Please, Maeve. For your mother's sake."

I gazed into my mother's eyes and saw the intense fear, pleading with me to go with her. She took my hand again, and this time, I didn't pull away. Mom went first, and I glanced at Quin before following the others into the darkness. Quin gave me a strangely conflicted look, then closed the basement door.

Halfway down the stairs, I snatched my hand back again and stopped.

"Maeve, what are you doing?" Mom frantically whispered.

I glanced up the stairs and saw a sliver of light coming from the bottom of the door. With my heart thumping wildly in my chest, I crept back up the stairs, stopping a few shy of the top, and crouching to see what was visible from the bottom of the door.

Heavy footsteps were entering the building, and I could soon see sets upon sets of black boots filing in and positioning themselves in insanely straight rows.

Then there was another pair of boots with a slower gait and heavier footfalls than the others. "Where is the boy?"

The grating voice once only inside my head now sounded throughout the entire upstairs. I immediately recognized it as Tarquin. He was here. And he had everything else I was after.

A hand touched my ankle. "Maeve," Mom whispered. "You need to come downstairs."

As scared as I was, I couldn't continue to the basement with the others. "Go," I told her. "I'll meet you there shortly."

"He hasn't come back," Otis said. "Neither of them has."

"Guy has not returned either?" Tarquin asked with an amused inflection in his voice. "Do you believe he has turned on us?"

"He had a soft spot for the boy," Otis said. "I couldn't say. All I know is you tasked him to return with Fin if he wished to retain his position and he has not yet returned."

"I grow tired of waiting. If Guy cannot complete the task, then I need someone who can." There was a long pause. "Quintiana, I task you with bringing Guy and the boy home. I want them both alive, so they can answer to me. And I want to be notified immediately upon their arrival. Is that understood?"

"Yes, sir," Quin said. It sounded like she was still standing close to the basement door.

"Good. You have forty-eight hours. I suggest you get to work." Another pause. "What other news do we have from the other side of the seam?"

"We're gathering intel on what the GBMA is planning next. Christi is under constant surveillance," Otis said.

The stairs creaked below me as Mom tried to inch closer to the basement. As soon as the noise sounded, she froze.

"Who's down there?" Tarquin asked.

"A few members replenishing supplies," Otis said. "Nothing to be alarmed about."

"Check it out," Tarquin demanded, and several sets of boots trotted toward the basement door.

I glanced down at Mom, whose eyes were wide with horror. There was no time to waste. I mouthed, "I love you," jumped to my feet and threw open the door before the soldiers could, making damn sure the focus was on me.

CHAPTER 35

*T*arquin eyed me almost gleefully as I emerged from the basement staircase. I slammed the door behind me and stood my ground as the soldiers immediately stopped their approach. In fact, everything in the room seemed to come to a blistering halt.

"The girl who refused to die," Tarquin said, his gravelly voice rubbing my nerves raw.

I could still hear him in my head, almost like his voice was everywhere—completely consuming.

"Sorry to disappoint you," I said—my whole body shaking, but my voice remaining steady. I couldn't show him how terrified I was. He had everything I'd come here to find. Two crystals hung from his neck —one of them presumably my father's—and a slice of the octagram tattoo was visible beneath his V-neck tee-shirt, confirming he did indeed have the needle. He also had a fancy dagger sheathed at his hip, which I now assumed was another Seam Dagger.

There were about ten soldiers in the room, and Tarquin gestured for them to return to their original positions as he took a few steps toward me, his footfalls heavy and calculated. "Otis, it seems you have some explaining to do," he said, stopping in the center of the room. "I'll deal with you shortly. But first, I have unfinished business with this one."

"I want my needle and my father's crystal back," I demanded. I wasn't going to get any points for cowering in his presence, and my confidence may even throw him off guard.

"It was always *my* needle," Tarquin said. "I'd been after that witch for far too long, especially after she silenced me. She didn't deserve a quick death. And neither do you."

So much for throwing him off.

Otis remained on the far side of the room, frozen in place. Quin and Storm stood near the wall, also not wanting to get in the middle of this. I truly was on my own—again.

The last crystal in my possession had been empty and I'd accomplished amazing feats. It proved that the power had come from me, not amplification from the crystal. And it always took an incredible amount of rage to bring that power to life… and there was no one I felt more rage toward than Tarquin—who haunted my dreams as the sewn man.

I felt the fire within me quickly build, a power radiating throughout my entire body. My hands began to burn, though they didn't glow like I'd seen with other people. It didn't matter; the flowing energy at my fingertips was all that mattered. Now I just needed singular focus and concentration... in a non-ideal environment like Professor Windsor had demonstrated. And like the craziness that took place in Professor Voltaire's office, this certainly wasn't ideal.

"Stay a while," Tarquin said, extending his arm to me.

I felt a heaviness fall over me, but it only lasted a few seconds. It drained as quickly as it had arrived.

While Tarquin looked momentarily perplexed, I gathered all the energy I had and shot a flaming ball at him. However, it stopped in midair halfway to him. Even the flames themselves stopped like they were frozen.

"So, you can resist freezing," Tarquin said. There was amusement in his tone.

I didn't know I'd resisted anything, but I wasn't going to let him know that. "You'll have to do better than that," I said, defiantly.

With another sweeping gesture, Tarquin launched the fireball back in my direction, which exploded on impact and threw me backward against the wall. And even though the ball exploded, the flames were not extinguished, and I screamed as they engulfed my clothes and continued to spread.

The background laughter barely registered as I dropped to the floor and rolled around to smother the flames. They spread from my clothes to my hair and all I could feel was searing pain. And still I screamed.

No one was throwing me a blanket or dousing me with water. Everyone else in the room was simply standing there, watching my life come to an agonizing end, as I flopped around on the floor like a tortured animal.

All I could hope was that the fire would burn through my nerves soon to extinguish the pain since I couldn't seem to extinguish the flames. My eyes couldn't even comprehend what was happening. I felt like my flesh was melting off my bones. Soon, I'd be nothing left but a stain on the floor.

If I could actually think clearly, maybe there was something else I could do to save myself—but the pain was too intense. No one would be able to concentrate under these excruciating conditions.

However, as I continued to frantically roll along the floor, the flames finally seemed to be dying down. Maybe my body had burned so much, it was losing fuel. Hell, if I knew. But the flames licking my face seemed to be dissipating.

I could finally see through the wall of fire. The

roaring in my ears was also subsiding. And my perception of the room slowly returned.

That was when I noticed Mom, now in a fight for her life with Tarquin. The other soldiers were still standing at attention in two separate lines, acting like a spectator ring around a schoolyard fight.

She came for me...

Beyond the rolling, I slapped at the few remaining flames threatening my body and finally killed them all. I was still in pain, but not as much as I would have expected after being inside an inferno. My clothing was scorched and full of holes, but the skin underneath seemed unharmed. I had assumed my face now looked like Freddie Krueger's, but when I brought a hand to my cheek, it felt smooth and cool to the touch. The hair that fell into my face also appeared undamaged.

WTF?

The only explanation I could think of was the protection spell from Professor Windsor, which I didn't think would extend past the Academy walls, let alone into Kicryria.

Not wanting to leave Mom alone in the fight one second longer, I jumped to my feet and surveyed the battle scene.

Mom collapsed to the ground after being kicked in the stomach. Otis had now entered the fight, but he was battling several of the soldiers, trying to break through the line to reach Tarquin. Quin and Storm remained on the sideline.

As Tarquin descended on Mom, I threw two more fireballs at him, which he didn't see until right before impact. Each of them exploded, but quickly fizzled out. He didn't catch fire like I had, remained on his feet, and quickly turned to me with a sadistic grin.

The ceiling above Tarquin began to crack and collapse in large chunks, but he batted away the debris with a swipe of energy—sending them toward Mom, forcing her to expend more energy on defense.

Tarquin unsheathed his dagger and gripped it tightly by his side as he slowly advanced on me.

Mom threw two soldiers aside who tried to hold her back, then rushed Tarquin from behind. She landed on his back, wrapped an arm around his neck, and squeezed. Tarquin heaved forward and flipped her over his head, and she landed on her back with a crunching thud.

I shot two more energy balls at him as he swung his arm down with the dagger. And at the same time, Otis broke free of the guards and rushed Tarquin from the side. He quickly became the more immediate threat, and Tarquin stopped his swing, elbowed Otis in the face, then slashed to the side as Otis ricocheted backwards. Before Otis could rebound out of range, the blade caught him in the throat and sliced it wide open.

Blood arced past the blade, spilling onto Mom and the floor around her as Otis continued to fall. He was as good as dead by the time his body hit and crumpled onto the floor.

Quin screamed and sprinted to him, dropping to his side and placing a hand over his gushing neck. He looked directly into her eyes, gurgling as more blood seeped over and around his lips.

Mom's foot shot up while she lay on her back, catching Tarquin right between the legs.

Fuckin' A, Mom!

He grunted and stumbled back a few steps, but still remained on his feet. While he recovered, I helped pull Mom up off the floor. She had tears in her eyes, glancing back at me, then over at Otis, whose expression now looked blank.

Quin was also on her feet. With a piercing cry, she removed the dagger from her hip and launched it at Tarquin. He threw his arm up in defense just as the blade sank into his bicep. And just as fast as it had stabbed him, it dislodged itself and was soaring back to Quin's outstretched hand.

Tarquin roared, turning toward his attacker. As Quin monopolized his attention, I noticed the crystals lift off Tarquin's neck. The chains snapped and flew toward Mom and me, though he managed to snatch one from the air.

Tarquin took another step back and gestured for his men to attack.

Four soldiers headed in our direction and Mom released a tidal wave of energy, knocking down two of them in the onslaught. The other two kept coming.

Mom dropped another soldier with a kick to the knee, then Quin slammed into the guy gunning for me, who then tripped over the body of a fallen comrade.

Tarquin hung back as several more soldiers advanced on us.

"Follow me!" Quin exclaimed, stepped in front of me, aimed for the closest soldier, and slashed the air between them.

I didn't know if everyone could see, but I immediately saw what she was doing. The magical blade cut through the air—through the universal fabric—and opened a gleaming seam. The seam extended through the air and right through the closest soldier, who cried out in horror as his body was cut in half, caught in a doorway between two worlds.

Quin pulled the seam wide and the soldier remained upright, with the halves of his body forced into awkward angles like some terrifying optical illusion. I had no idea what would happen to him if the seam were to be sewn up, and I sure as hell didn't want to see it.

"Run!" Quin yelled and shoved me forward.

"Mom, let's go!" I yelled, just before jumping into the abyss, through the seam, and landing outside the crumbling house we'd first arrived in.

Mom dove through next, followed by Quin, who then ran past both of us into the house, aiming for the wall hiding the secret seam.

"The seam needs to be closed," Mom said, slamming the door behind her. It barely remained on the hinges and wouldn't lock, so Mom threw her weight against the door to hold it in place. "What are we doing?"

"Escaping," Quin said, dropping to her knees by the wall, unspooling the red thread, and forcing the seam in the wall to open.

There was a crash against the door, almost knocking Mom to the ground. But she dug her heels in and continued to apply as much pressure as she could.

I ran back to help as a soldier crashed through one of the broken windows. I skidded to a stop, glanced at a fallen chair by the window and saw it attack him in my mind. With only a second delay, the chair slid across the floor like a demon and slammed into the unsuspecting soldier.

Mom pushed off the door, which now looked securely set within the frame—some other magical feat she must have performed while the soldiers outside were banging on it.

"Let's go!" Quin called to us.

The soldier who got hit by the chair was still finding his balance when Mom hit him with another wall of energy, tossing him back out the window like a ragdoll.

Mom and I ran to the seam in the wall with the crisscrossing red thread.

"Don't pull out any of the string or we're screwed," Quin said and urged us to enter the void.

"Go, Mom," I said. "I'll be right behind you."

"You should go—"

"This isn't the time to freakin' argue!"

"Go or I'm leaving you both here!" Quin yelled.

Mom reluctantly agreed and carefully stepped through the seam. I was about to follow her when the door exploded into thousands of wood and metal fragments and projectiles. Four soldiers stormed into the house. Haloed in dust just outside the doorframe, stood Tarquin. I was unable to make out any specific features as he stood amid the murky cloud, but the silhouette was enough for me to know it was him.

I didn't waste another second before stepping into the void, careful to not dislodge the red trip-wires. Quin was right behind me with the spool of thread in her hand.

She frantically pulled at the thread to close the seam. Mom and I watched wide-eyed as the shimmering gash in the wall shrank to nothing, until the plaster appeared to be fusing itself back together.

Then all that was left was the single point at the bottom of the wall where the thread was still connected.

Quin yanked at the last of the thread and it disconnected from the wall. The phone cord that had also been connected to the wall fell to the ground, one end of it severed.

"There," Quin said. "They can't follow us through *that* door. But they can make a new one if Tarquin's desperate enough. The safest thing to do is get back to the Academy."

"What happened to Storm?" I asked.

"He didn't break his cover," Quin said.

"Is that going to matter now? Tarquin doesn't seem like the most reasonable and stable guy."

"I pray he'll be okay." Quin headed straight for the back door like she knew the routine of this safe-house. Of course, she did. If she really was Otis's daughter, then she'd probably been here countless times before. She may have even lived here with him. But I knew better than to ask her about it now.

As we made our way back to the Academy, the air felt colder than ever—especially with the holes in my clothes. I may have to finally retire my leather jacket, which had been with me through a lot of shit. Being set on fire might have been her limit.

It wasn't until the Spellcrest Academy gate was in view that I started to fear my mother wouldn't be allowed in. I didn't know much about the protective spell, but it was designed to keep unwanted people out, though it wasn't infallible—as proved by the incident in the Crystal Crypt last trimester.

I didn't voice my concerns. I was sure Quin knew a thing or two about the Academy and she didn't seem concerned.

I held my breath as we reached the gate and didn't let it out until the three of us were safely through. Now it was my turn to lead them the rest of the way.

CHAPTER 36

I opened the door to my room and flipped on the light. Finley's alarm hadn't gone off yet for him to get up and shower, but our arrival would certainly provide that wake-up call.

His eyes opened, somewhat confused as his eyesight had to adjust to the light. But then he saw Quin, whom I assumed he knew—then his gaze landed on Mom. Finley's eyes grew wide and he rose to a seated position on the bed, letting his legs dangle over the edge.

"Finley…" she said, her eyes glossy with more tears. Mom tentatively approached the bed, clearly heartbroken at the sight of his mouth being sewn shut. It had taken me days to get used to it.

From the look on his face, I assumed this was the first time Finley was seeing her too. Guy had probably told Finley that she'd been brought back the last time he was here, which would explain him gifting the empty crystal. Finley had tears streaming down his face as Mom sat down on the bed and embraced him.

I let them have their moment, then approached, knelt on the floor, and wrapped my arms around both of them. And the three of us cried together—tears of sadness for everything we'd been through, everything we'd lost, as well as tears of joy and gratitude for being reunited in this crazy world after one hell of a decade. The only one we were missing now was Dad, but I was hopeful one day soon our family hug would be a foursome again.

There were so many questions I had for Mom concerning her and Dad's roles in all of this, but for right now, none of that mattered. What mattered most was having her back, and I wanted to revel in that euphoric feeling for a little while longer.

I glanced over at Quin, who was now sitting in my desk chair, eyeliner streaked down her cheeks. Blood was caked on her hands and arms, along with splotches on her clothes. She was a mess and looked like she needed a hug too. It wasn't going to be me who gave it to her, but I felt someone should. I'd been given my mother back, but she'd just lost her father. As much as anyone, I knew how hard that was.

I stood and stepped back from the bed where Mom and Finley were still interlocked. "Thank you for what you did back there," I said to Quin. "You saved all of our butts... And I'm sorry for what happened." I didn't want to specifically mention Otis, so I hoped she simply understood.

"It happened so fast," she said, looking past me. "I thought I could save him... but I couldn't stop the bleeding."

Mom extended an arm and waved Quin over. "Come here, sweetie."

It didn't take much for Quin to comply, and she joined Mom and Finley on the bed, where another group hug commenced. It allowed Quin to fully let out her anguish as well, something we all needed after the night we'd had. Strangely, she looked right at home in my family's arms, to the point I almost felt like the outsider.

After a minute, Quin let go and stood a few feet from me. Neither of us seemed to know how to get comfortable in this new dynamic. I didn't know anything about her besides Otis being her father. I didn't know if her mother was still out there, if she had other siblings, or if she was it—the last of her family. All things that would come up soon, but not tonight.

Mom pulled out the crystal she'd stolen from Tarquin and held it in her palm. It didn't glow, and I immediately feared the worst. She held the gem up to eyelevel, and her expression sank further.

"It's not him, is it?" I asked, prepared for the disappointing answer that inevitably followed.

"It's empty," she said, sorrowfully. "Tarquin must have snatched back your father."

"Then we have one more reason to confront him again," I said.

Mom stared glumly at the crystal in her hand. "The cost might be even higher next time," she said and began to cry again.

Is she crying for Otis? I wanted to ask, but not in front of Quin.

"Then we'll pay it." I glanced at Quin and she nodded with vengeful resolve.

I needed to learn more about what was going on, so I could be better prepared. If I was going to face Tarquin again, then I needed to train harder than ever before. And most of all, we needed more help. It was time to finally bring Devon on board, tell him everything, and see what resources he could provide.

We had to prepare for the worst. We were going to war.

EPILOGUE: DEVON

I sat down at the computer with a quick breakfast I'd grabbed from the cafeteria and fast forwarded through the recording of the last day. I loved watching Maeve in her natural state, as well as the compassion she had for her brother even after everything that had happened in recent months. I was falling hard for this girl, which made what I was required to do that much harder.

"You hungry, big guy?" I asked, but there was no reply. I guessed he didn't find the question funny anymore.

I slowed the recording when I noticed Maeve get into bed without changing into her pajamas, wanting to make sure I was seeing it right. She was up to something again—and sure enough, at ten minutes 'til midnight, she jumped out of bed, donned her leather jacket and snuck out of the room. Obviously, I lost her after that, so I fast-forwarded again, and she returned a little before 2 a.m., but she didn't enter her room alone.

I intently watched the laptop screen, trying to make out who had entered the room with her. There was a blond woman with shoulder length hair dressed in short sleeves and black pants. Behind her entered a black-haired teenager in a blue tank top, a girl I felt I'd seen before. Did she attend the Academy? Or had she graduated in the last year or two? She looked familiar, but I couldn't exactly place her.

Finley awoke as they filed into the small room. With his lips sewn shut, it was hard to fully read his expression, but it was clear he knew at least one of them. The woman sat beside him on the bed and gave him a heartbreaking hug.

"What am I seeing here?" I asked.

"I don't know. I can't see your screen, *idiot*."

So, he is awake.

I unplugged the power cable, picked up the computer, then walked it across the room. I stopped before the energy shield and held up the computer, the screen facing into the makeshift cell. The view through the energy shield resembled looking through a thin waterfall, so it wasn't clear, but he'd be able to see well enough.

"Who are they?" I demanded.

"Why should I tell you?" Guy asked, defiantly.

"You're the one with the great intel. You tell me, smart guy."

It took minimal energy to force him into the shield, which zapped him like being hit with a taser and dropped his body to the floor in a spastic heap.

"Real mature," Guy said after regaining a majority of his faculties. "That's how you get what you want."

"Just tell me who they are," I repeated.

"That's their mother," Guy finally said. "And the girl's a friend of mine."

"Maeve's mother? She was crystallized."

"And now she's not. You know how that works. They tell you about it in Theory of Necromancy. Or were you not paying attention 'cause you had more important things to do?"

"But Finley looked like he recognized her from the moment he saw her."

"A little family blood goes a long way." Guy laughed, then fell into a coughing fit.

"That's what you used Maeve's blood for? You brought back her mother—the *real* her?"

"Now you're the one sounding like a Norm. You should hear yourself. And you know you're not gonna be able to talk your way out of this one, right? You won't be able to hold onto her once she finds out you've been spying on her for your mother."

"I can be *very* persuasive."

"You really are an idiot."

"Then I'll just have to make sure she doesn't find out," I said and walked the laptop back to the desk. "Some things have to be done for the greater good. Duty over love. It got us you, didn't it?"

"Yeah; you got me. Congratulations. You're a real bona fide hero," Guy said sarcastically, finally picking himself up off the floor. He mockingly clapped his hands as he returned to his cot and sat down. "I can't wait to see that firecracker kick your ass."

"Maybe I'll let her kick *your* ass first," I said, closing the screen of the laptop. "Time to say *good morning* and see what's really going on." I headed for the door but gave him a quick glance back. "Don't go anywhere."

Ready for the next part of Maeve's story?

Continue now with Crystallize!

AFTER THE FINAL WORD

JUNE 24, 2019

I first and foremost want to thank you for reading *Crestfallen*, and now you're even continuing with the author's note! I'm so grateful and could obviously not do this without you.

This book has been an interesting adventure and experiment for me because it is the first one I've done without the aid of an outline. I didn't even write down any notes. I started with a few major plot points I needed to hit, where the story would end, then simply started writing.

It was scary. There were multiple times I thought I was writing myself into a wall, fearing I'd have to backtrack and scrap hundreds or thousands of words. For an indie author like myself trying to release faster, that would be terribly inefficient. And as I write against the clock, I can't afford to be inefficient.

However, the story was also an adventure because I was discovering it and learning new things about the characters in real time. I usually get a sense of discovery since my outlines aren't terribly detailed, but I'd never experienced it to this extent.

This story very much felt like driving along a dark and windy road, only being able to see to the reach of the headlights. The rest of the world was a mystery, but as the car continued to move forward, small sections of the mystery were revealed.

For example, (*WAIT! If you skipped to this section without reading the story first, then stop reading now to avoid spoilers*) the revealed relationship between Maeve's mother and Otis didn't come to me until I was writing the climax. I got an idea I hadn't considered before and decided to run with it. To be fair, once I came up with the idea, I gave it a lot of thought and slept on it. I was still excited about the revelation the next day, so at that point, I knew it was a true part of the story.

Even thought there was an excitement to the writing process of this story, it's not something I want to repeat in the near future. I'd rather be more prepared going into the next book.

My outline doesn't have to be that elaborate. I don't need to see all the detail beyond the beams of the headlights. But at least I'll have the navigation running. If needed, I can always take an unexpected turn and the navigation will be forced to adjust.

A few unexpected turns are good for me too. They keep the story fresh. And I want a fresh story. A fun story. A thrilling story. And a story you'll be compelled to revisit.

I don't know if I've accomplished that, but it's the ultimate goal with every story I write.

I would love to keep Maeve's story going, and for that, I need *your* help. If you enjoyed the book, then please leave a review, and tell your friends and the strangers standing in line with you at Starbucks (or insert favorite coffee shop here). Reviews and word of mouth are the best ways to support authors you love.

Thank you again, and I look forward to seeing you in the next story.

Semper Prorsum,
Michael Pierce

P.S. Here's the link to Review Crestfallen on Amazon.

ABOUT THE AUTHOR

Michael Pierce loves stories that are thrilling and unexpected, romantic and fantastical—addictive tales that will keep you reading long past the witching hour.

He currently lives in Southern California with his wife, kids, and two blood-thirsty chiweenies.

When he's not at the computer, he enjoys spending quality time with family, practicing yoga, playing guitar behind closed doors, and listening to audiobooks.

Connect with him online:
michaelpierceauthor.com
michael@michaelpierceauthor.com

Made in the USA
Monee, IL
03 November 2019

16278743R00189